Also by J. J. Dutra

Nautical Twilight
The Fishermen's Ball

Archway Publishing books may be ordered through booksellers or by contacting:

Archway Publishing
1663 Liberty Drive
Bloomington, IN 47403
www.archwaypublishing.com
1 (888) 242-5904

ISBN: 978-1-4808-6927-1 (sc)
ISBN: 978-1-4808-6928-8 (e)

Library of Congress Control Number: 2018959955

Print information available on the last page.

Archway Publishing rev. date: 11/06/2018

DEAD LOW TIDE

J. J. DUTRA

ARCHWAY
PUBLISHING

This book is dedicated to David, always in my heart

It would not have been possible to write this book without information provided by *The Provincetown Banner Archives, The Cape Cod Times Archives, The Provincetown Portuguese Festival Committee, The Provincetown Historic Committee, The Provincetown Fishermen's Association and the Truro and Provincetown Libraries.* Thank you for keeping our history alive.

Many thanks to first readers: Bev Phaneuf, Angela Caruso, Ellen Ryder, and Randy Trullo. Thank you for reading, making suggestions and cheering me on. Thank you Nancy Bloom, friend, photographer, and teacher, for the cover photo of Provincetown, for the author photo, and for your technical support. Thank you to my family, you guys are the best: Jackson, Bob, Nicole, Susie, Olivia, Ryan, and Alex. To my extended family: Shawn, Colleen, Sara, Krissy, Mary, Bobby G, Jackie and Marty, Peter, thanks for the memories.

And where would a book be without the support of my readers: Thank you to the many friends for sending letters, emails, and for sharing your wonderful stories. God Speed and Fair Winds.

*"The quality of mercy is not strained, it droppeth as the gentle rain from heaven upon the place beneath. It is twice blessed. It blesseth him that gives and him that takes ………
It is an attribute to God himself when mercy seasons justice."*
Wm Shakespeare, The Merchant of Venice

Prologue

Clouds obscured the stars, shading any luminance the night could offer, creating a world of shadows. There were no overhead lights along this stretch of road. If a person was heading out of town at two o'clock in the morning and if they strained their eyes, they would detect an outline of woods on the left side of the road. Beyond the oaks and scrub pine, hills of dunes rose and fell until they met the Atlantic Ocean.

Rocks formed a jagged breakwater on the right side of road. Slippery and perilous, these granite boulders could sparkle in sunshine as well as hold back the sea in darkness. The Army Corp of Engineers had placed them there in order to keep the water from flooding the road when a storm surge pushed the bay onto the shore. They were built up, stacked, and banked against the land.

The headlamps from a Ford pickup truck cast glowing circles across the black pavement. The vehicle slowed and pulled to the side, touching dirt and sand. All lights were extinguished. It had stopped half a mile past the last house on Old County Road, the only road out of town. If the vehicle had continued it would have gone all the way to Boston passing through Truro, Wellfleet, Eastham and dozens of other communities along its path.

The sound of peepers from nearby ponds could be heard and the June night air carried the smell of salt and seaweed. Inside the Ford's cab the only sound was rapid breathing. No words were spoken. It was as if their task had been prearranged, planned, and discussed, although it had not. Yet somehow, they knew what had to be done. This was the kind of work for which there were no instructions and no preparation.

It was a chance they needed to take. Two doors opened at

the same time as if by some silent signal and then closed without adding to the quiet night. No footfalls could be heard as they stepped from the truck to the soft sand.

The tailgate was lowered revealing a cylinder seven feet long, resembling a log, but was just an old rug rolled up. And yet, if one looked closely, the black soles from a pair of shoes would be visible.

They worked together pulling and tugging their cargo until the load fell out of the truck and lay on the ground at their feet. Maneuvering the heavy mass, they dragged it across the dirt to the top of the embankment where the breakwater began and then fell sixteen feet to the bottom. Their breath came in loud bursts. They each grabbed an end of the bundle. Struggling to get to the edge of the embankment, the pair moved with uncoordinated effort, but in unison. And then with a burst of strength and energy, they lifted, shook, and firmly unrolled the rug. It spun out, opening as it went down the sloping granite stones, presenting a body that jerked, bounced and then slid its way across the slimy rocks. It landed unceremoniously like a Raggedy-Ann-Doll, on hard packed wet sand. It was dead low tide.

Chapter 1

James Crowley finished his breakfast at Betty's Luncheonette. The café contained six tables and a counter with ten stools, all of them taken. The door opened, and a man stepped in. Crowley thought Lewis looked more nervous than usual, kind of jumpy and out of breath, as if he'd run the entire block from the police station. The chief liked the kid for his quick wit, eagerness, and knowledge of the fishing community.

"Chief, you'd better come." The officer was boisterous. His head was bouncing to one side as if he were clearing water out his ear. Everyone stopped eating and looked at the two men. Crowley put fifty cents on the counter, thanked Betty, and picked up his hat. He looked more like a professor than the Provincetown police chief.

Chief Crowley hated wearing his uniform. The wool made him itch. He wore it only when reporting to the board of selectmen, meeting with other Cape Cod officials, or when attending funerals. His usual attire was dark pants, a white shirt, and a dark-blue jacket or sweater. But it didn't matter what he wore; everyone in town knew who he was. The chief turned to the patrolman. "Let's talk outside."

Much to the chagrin of the luncheonette clients, the Provincetown policemen turned away from the counter, leaving the *Cape Cod Standard Times* open with headlines that read "Effort to Lift Siege Blocked" and the date June 2, 1938. Outside the café, the town was quiet. A delivery van, two bikes, and the PPD squad car were parked in front of the restaurant. The June sky was cerulean.

"Looks like you have everyone at Betty's wondering what's

going on, including me." The chief walked to the car, smiled at Lewis, and then opened the door of a black '37 Chevy sedan.

The chief had argued in favor of an upgrade for the police car for three consecutive years before the selectmen finally agreed to put it on the town budget last year.

"Well, what seems to be the problem?" The chief was not expecting to hear about dead bodies, but that was exactly what Lewis said.

"There's a body washed up in front of Miss Alter's house, east end of town." The young officer couldn't hold still. "She called the station. I ran right over to get you."

"Okay Lewis, get in. Where does Miss Alter live?" the chief asked as he put the key into the ignition. "Did you make a note of the time she called before you ran out the door? And did you lock up the station?"

Lewis had a habit of leaving everything unlocked—car door, house door, and the police station. Last winter the chief had entered his office and found Katarina Bateman sitting at his desk. The old woman said she was waiting to tell him that her granddaughter had just graduated from Harvard University and was in town for a few days. Mrs. Bateman thought it would be nice if the chief asked her out on a date. She told him that his was the only comfortable chair she could find in the police station and she had tried them all. The chief thought she sounded like Goldilocks.

He had thanked Mrs. Bateman for her interest in his love life, adding that at this time he was too busy with town business to consider dating. "But I am interested in how you got into my office." The grandmother told him that the door was open, so she decided to wait.

Lewis spoke up, "All right, one mistake and I'll never hear the end of it. Yes, I locked the front door. Miss Alter lives on Commercial Street, at the foot of Allerton. I told her to sit tight. We'd be right there."

It took less than five minutes to get to the house. The chief drove a little faster than usual. They passed Jimmy Peete, who raised his hand in greeting. He was situated on the cart holding the reins of his horse, heading back to his farm in Truro after unloading his strawberries to local markets. Crowley turned right on Allerton, the last cross street before leaving town. The house was white with black shutters. Most houses in Provincetown had been built between 1720 and 1850. This one appeared newer, with dormers and a roof that was shapely. The chief thought it was called a gambrel roof. Newer homes were constantly being added. The town was spreading like spilled honey.

An oak front door with glass windowpanes on each side was opened before the two policemen had time to knock.

"I'm so glad you're here," the woman said. She stepped back to allow them to enter a wide hall.

The chief removed his hat. "Are you Sara Alter?"

"Yes. Yes. This way." The house was sparsely furnished. They entered a large room with windows facing the bay. They walked across the room following the woman, who was talking and pointing. "It was such a lovely morning that I decided to take my coffee outside on the deck." Miss Alter opened a door at the center of the windows and pointed. She did not step out.

The two policemen moved to the deck, looked over the railing, and spotted the body. It was lying facedown, head and shoulders on the sand, legs in the water. "Lewis, what time is high tide?" The chief was walking to the stairs that led to the beach.

"I believe the tide's still coming in." Lewis kept an eye on the weather, the boats, and fishing information. Whenever the chief had a marine-related question, Crowley knew he could count on Lewis.

The chief was yelling as he started down the outside stairs. "Ask Miss Alter if you can use her phone. Call Dr. Rice and Mr. Richland. Tell them to get over here as quickly as possible. Tell them tide and time wait for no man." Lewis was already headed back inside to make the phone calls. Crowley hurried down the wooden stairs.

The corpse was a man. His face was half buried in the sand. His dark hair lay flattened against his head, matted with seaweed. He had on black pants, black shoes, and a plaid shirt. Chief Crowley knelt and touched the side of the man's neck. He felt ice cold. The body was swollen with water and had the color of a gray sky on a winter's day. There was no pulse.

Stepping closer to the water's edge while scanning the body, Crowley felt his feet sink in the sand and water seep into his shoes. "Damn," he said. He wasn't sure if it was because of the dead man or his wet feet, but he said it again: "Damn."

The chief's eyes stopped at a rip in the man's shirt. He touched the tear in the cloth and noticed a large gash in the man's skin beneath it. Crowley didn't want to jump to conclusions, but there was a large wound in his back.

Lewis appeared at the railing above the chief and called to his boss. "Doc Rice was out. His wife said she would call him. I told her to have the doc meet us at Richland's. Mr. Richland is on his way. I told him to bring the hearse and someone to help." The patrolman continued talking as he descended the stairs to the beach. "He said he'd be here in ten minutes." He stopped speaking and stood next to the police chief.

"Good. Any longer and we'll have to drag the body up the beach, and I'd rather we didn't have to do that," Crowley said. "If Richland doesn't get here soon the corpse will be floating." The police chief continued as he squatted next to the dead man, "There's no blood. The water took care of that. Hard to say how long he's been dead." He looked at Lewis. "There's a gash in his back." Crowley pointed to the area but didn't touch the shirt again. "We'll get a better look when he's at the funeral home."

Crowley stood and arched his back, pulling his shoulder blades together to stretch his upper torso. He turned to Lewis. "Help me roll him on his side so we can see his face." They crouched together and pulled the body toward them. "I don't recognize him. Is he anyone you know?"

Lewis shook his head without answering, gawking at the soggy, puffy mass.

"If you feel you will throw up, please don't do it near the body." Lewis shook his head, stood up, and walked toward the house. The chief patted all the pockets in the man's pants and shirt. They appeared empty. He gently moved the man back down onto the sand, into the same position they had found him in.

Crowley stood up and walked the beach for a few feet around the body. He was looking at the sand. There were footprints from the house to where he stood. He recognized the small footprints of Miss Alter coming from her stairway. Lewis had left long prints, large size, where he had dug in as if running. His own footprints were close to the body. The tide had pretty much wiped the beach clean of anything else.

The chief noted one odd thing about the man. His socks were pulled up over his pants.

"Feeling better?" Crowley asked as Lewis retuned to his side. No answer was required. The chief scanned the horizon, left to right, and then out into the bay. The water was sparkling like diamonds in the sunshine.

"The current runs in a semicircle around the bay, coming in from the east, flowing west around the bay every six hours. Is that right?" The chief spoke as he waved his arm toward the open water, motioning in a counterclockwise direction.

Lewis answered, "Then back out in the opposite direction. We have big tides, ten feet yesterday."

"So the question is, how did this man end up in front of Miss Alter's house?" The chief's eyes followed the shoreline around toward the hills and cliffs of Truro. "He may have gone into the water up that way or washed in from somewhere out in the bay."

"I'll need to know the time of the tides last night and for a couple of days previous." The chief looked up at the house, not searching for answers there, but to rest his eyes from the glare off the water. He could see the ceiling in the living area and the bottom of the deck that protruded from it.

"Also, get me a book about the currents. Maybe we can get a better handle on where this man went into the water. And hopefully Doc Rice will be able to give us the time of death." Crowley wiped his damp hands on his pants and then took a notebook from his shirt pocket. Realizing that his hands were too wet to use the paper, he returned it.

Lewis spoke up, "Maybe he fell from a boat and drifted in."

"That's a possibility," the chief said, "But there have been no reports of a missing boater, passenger," he paused, "fisherman or local citizen."

The chief looked down at the body. "He's wearing dress shoes. And look at the socks. They are partially pulled up over the pants," Crowley said.

Cape Cod citizens live with the fact that as the weather warms boat traffic picks up and tourists outnumbered the locals by thousands. The chief continued, "The Boston ferry is running and I've seen a few transient vessels. There are yachts coming and going in the harbor at this time of year."

Crowley asked the patrolman to call the Cape's harbormasters. "Find out if there are any reports of a missing man in the past few days. Maybe we'll get lucky."

A door opened above them and Mr. Richland from the funeral home stepped onto the deck. He picked up his hand to acknowledge the chief.

"Down here," Crowley called. "Have your men bring the

stretcher around the side of the building. There's no need to go through the house."

The chief turned to Lewis and said, "Wait here and give the funeral director a hand. After the man is loaded into the hearse stay in the squad car and wait for me. I want to have a word with Miss Alter."

Chief Crowley was offered coffee. He shook his head, "Thank you, but no, maybe another time." Miss Alter appeared to be in her fifties. Her hair was pinned up on top of her head and a pair of glasses hung from a pink ribbon around her neck.

The room took full advantage of the water view. A deck extended out, over the sand, obscuring the sight of the men removing the body. "You have a nice home, Miss Alter" The chief felt the need to put the woman at ease.

"It's Mrs. Alter. My husband died four years ago and I moved to this house last year."

Chief Crowley nodded and said he was sorry for her loss. "I need to ask you a few questions. Would you mind?" His voice softened. "Do you live alone?"

She nodded in the affirmative. "Please have a seat," she said. When they were settled she continued, "I'm alone at the moment but my niece will be arriving tonight." Her mouth gave a quick smile at the thought. "My husband and I spent summers here. Things changed." Her thoughts turned inward. It was silent in the room.

"Now I stay year round." She looked toward the windows at the bright sky and sparkling water. "Somehow the view soothes me. Well, until today." She shook her head. Tendrils of hair fell into her face and she wound them around her ear. "This has been very disturbing. I've never seen anything like that. He was rolling around in the water, sloshing from side to side. At first I thought it was a dead seal or whale."

Chief Crowley said he understood. "I'm sorry you had

to witness this. You went down to the beach? Did you touch anything?"

"I was on the balcony. I went to the phone as soon as I realized it was a man. Tillie the operator connected me to your office and I spoke to that nice young man. Then I ran down to the beach. I bent to touch him, but I didn't. I mean I couldn't touch him." Mrs. Alter shivered. "After seeing him close up, I just couldn't. I knew he was dead as soon as I saw him."

Her body shivered. She wrapped her arms across her chest and put her hands under her arms, pulling in for warmth as if she'd just stepped into a winter storm. "I could only see part of his face, the rest was in the sand. The way he was moving in the water, so unnatural. I didn't want to leave him there, but what could I do. So I ran back upstairs, watched from the deck and waited for you." The chief made a note and nodded. She added, "I hope that was alright?"

"Yes of coarse it's okay." The chief stood up, put his notebook in his pocket, and thanked Mrs. Alter. He looked out toward the water then turned and said, "Please let me know if there is anything our department can do for you. And I may need to speak to you again." Crowley looked at her for a moment, wondering if there were any other questions he should ask. He told her that he would be in touch and left. The body was already gone.

Chapter 2

They went directly to the station. The phone was ringing when Lewis unlocked the door. The chief headed to his office while Lewis answered the phone, "Provincetown Police Department."

The desk and chair in the chief's office had belonged to his father and Crowley was very fond of it. He looked at it with longing. Opposite the desk two captain's chairs waited for occupancy. They had armrests and had come from his aunt's dining room. A corkboard was perched on a rectangle table, leaning against the far wall. Crowley used the board for notices of town committee meetings, the occasional postcard, and interesting newspaper articles. The chief turned the board over revealing a blank side. He would place all the information gathered regarding the case on index cards and tack them to the board.

The basement office had no windows. There were two doors. One led to the hall and the other to a closet with a bathroom. The bathroom contained a gun cabinet along with foul weather gear, galoshes to slip over shoes, a bucket, mop, office supplies, and a change of clothing. Experience had taught Crowley that it was simpler and less time consuming to keep extras of everything at the office.

The chief looked down at his pants and shook his head. The cuffs were soaking wet. He rolled them up and slipped out of his shoes. He pulled a pair of socks from his desk drawer and was putting them on when Lewis walked in. "That was Dr. Rice on the phone. He's at Richland's. He said for you to come take a look."

"Thanks Lewis. I'm on my way. Should anyone call, write it down and tell them I'll get back to them. Get those tide charts please, and find the phone number and schedule for the ferry." The chief stood up and they left the office. "If anyone calls about a missing man, get their name, address and how they can be reached. Got it? Let's keep this under our hats for now."

Lewis went back to the counter and sat at his desk. He found his copy of *Eldridge's Tide and Pilot Book,* a comprehensive listing of tides from Maine to New Jersey, and began thumbing through the book. He didn't have a chart of the area, but he knew where he could find one. He picked up the phone and called his cousin Manual Macara who owned the fishing boat, *Victory.* He would get a chart of Cape Cod Bay from him.

The Chief arrived at Richland's Funeral Home and parked next to Dr. Rice's car at the back of the building. The home had living quarters on the second and third floors, viewing rooms on the first, and a basement reserved for the deceased. The chief walked down the stairs and into what Mr. Richland jokingly called "God's waiting room." The floors, ceiling and walls had recently been whitewashed. A whiff of paint mixed with the odor of formaldehyde made the chief feel queasy.

"Looks like you have yourself another mystery," said the jovial Doctor Rice. "But I think you may have already surmised that. He's got a rather large wound in his back." Doctor Rice stopped. His bushy eyebrows came together and he shook his head. He continued, "I thought that we were finished with this sort of thing when that murdering Suvera met his maker."

The doctor was referring to the man who had been tossed into the frigid Atlantic waters and torn apart by a propeller during a foiled plan to murder Mary Diogo last January. A joint effort of local, state, and federal agencies led to the rescue of the young woman. "I hoped that was the end of evil in this town," Dr. Rice said, "wishful thinking on my part."

The doctor had rosy cheeks and white bushy hair. If he had a beard he would look like Santa Claus. People felt comfortable around him. Rice had been the town doctor for as long as Crowley could remember. James felt he could talk to the doctor about almost anything, things he couldn't tell anyone else, feelings, fears, and memories.

Rice continued, "It's a stab wound. Entering through the forth-intercostal space from the back, deep, wide, it went straight into the heart. I believe the weapon was long and fairly wide. I'll measure the area and let you know exactly. He didn't stand a chance. He would have bled out within minutes. Nothing could have saved him."

The doctor had a black rubber apron over his clothing like the fishermen wear when filleting fish or cut scallops. He also wore rubber gloves, galoshes over his shoes, and had a sun visor on his forehead. He looked as if her were a mix of card dealer, blacksmith, and fisherman, and yet he was a man recognized wherever he went as the best doctor in town.

The chief nodded toward Mr. Richland who stood at the back of the room preparing another body. Crowley directed his question to the mortician, a tall balding man who wore a white apron like a baker or a butcher. "Who's that?" Crowley asked.

"Mr. Alves, ninety-two years old, died last night at home in his sleep. Doc Rice can verify. Nothing for you to worry about," the mortician replied. The Town Hall has a certificate. Your office will get a copy."

Crowley turned his attention back to the doctor who was pulling off the rubber gloves. "Can you to give me a time of death?" Crowley asked.

"Hard to pin-point the exact time because he's been in saltwater for quite a while. From the condition of the skin, I'd say he's been in the briny deep for at least a day, maybe more. But I can tell you that he was dead before he went into the water. There are no bruises or contusions on the body, just that large rip in his back. The water left him bloated, but he's mostly intact. I'll get you a written report as soon as I can."

"Thanks doc," Crowley said. "I'd like to take a look at the

wound and then his belongings." Doctor Rice put the gloves back on. The chief continued, "I take it you've called the county medical examiner? All suspicious deaths are reported."

Rice looked up at the ceiling and then he rolled the man toward him. "Yes. Of coarse I called. Now look here. You can see how wide the wound is. It's not the kind of slice a knife would make. It had to be something wider, thicker. In my limited experience, I'd say not a knife." The doctor raised his head so he could see Crowley from under his visor. He continued, "I don't know what, yet. But I'll figure it out. You know I enjoy a challenge." He winked at the chief. Crowley tried not to laugh.

The doctor turned the corpse onto its stomach. Crowley watched as he used an instrument to probe the site. "The angle of the wound is straight in, a little unusual. If the murderer came in from behind, the wound would have a downward trajectory." The doctor demonstrated by using his empty hand. His arm came down. "If I hold the weapon so that it goes in straight, it's an awkward movement."

After the doctor had placed the body onto his back and covered it with a clean white sheet he said, "Turn around and stand still." The doctor stepped close to the chief as if he was going to hug him. He then reached around the policeman, and planted his fist firmly, but without vigor on the chief's back, between the shoulder blades and close to the spine. It was awkward. "Would you care to dance?" the doc said.

The chief ignored him. Crowley was over six feet tall and the doctor was just able to reach around so that his fist struck the chief's back. "The weapon goes in like this." The men stepped apart. "See what I mean?"

The doctor wasn't finished. He walked around the chief. "Now, if I come up behind you and strike your back, I'd have to be very short to drive the weapon straight in and even then, there's a slight downward motion."

Doctor Rice now faced the chief. He continued, "Of course there is the possibility that the murderer held the knife by the handle and drove it in this way." The doctor turned his wrist so that his fingers were on the top and pushed outward. "Like a lunge when fencing, it's still a bit clumsy." The doctor removed his visor. "I'll leave it to you, you're the policeman."

Crowley didn't move. It was silent in the room for a moment. He looked at the covered body. Then the chief added, "Maybe the man fell onto his back and struck something. Or perhaps the victim was lying down, maybe asleep when he was stabbed."

Doc Rice nodded, he pursed his lips, and rubbed his chin. "Good point, I'll give it more thought. But keep in mind I don't think it is a knife wound."

"Thanks Doc. You always help," the chief said.

Crowley walked across the room to the undertaker. "I'd like to see his clothing and personal items."

Mr. Richland took a cardboard box from a shelf and set it on an unoccupied table. "Everything is in here," the mortician said. "He didn't have much."

Chief Crowley took the items out of the box one at a time. The clothes were wet, damp but no longer soaking. He searched the pockets of the pants. They were empty. A label read *Sears Roebuck Co* inside the collar of the plaid flannel shirt. It was unraveling where it had been torn by the weapon. Suspenders were wound in a loose ball alongside socks, shoes, and undergarments.

"That's it?" Crowley looked at the bottom of the empty box then up at Mr. Richland. "No wallet, keys, or change?"

"Yes sir, I mean no chief. That's all the man had. Like I said, not much." The funeral director stepped back and cocked his head in the direction of the body belonging to Mr. Alves. "I'd like to get back to work. Is there anything else?" Mr. Richland waited.

The chief shook his head and replied, "Sorry to hear about Mr. Alves. He was a surveyor wasn't he? Worked at Town Hall?"

"Yes, but not for years. He had a big family, wife is deceased, but he has four boys and a girl, many grandchildren and great-grandchildren. It'll be a big funeral. The wake is tomorrow night if you can make it."

"Thanks, I'll try to put in an appearance." The chief walked to the door. "I'll be at the station, doc. Stop by when you're finished here, I won't keep you long." The chief looked back at the doctor. "By the way, what's that thing you've been wearing on your head?"

The doctor laughed, "You like it? My son brought it back from New York. I was told it is used by the card dealers. I like the way it shades my eyes from the overhead lights when I'm doing close work like putting in stitches, pulling out glass or metal fragment. I've found it most helpful."

"Good idea." Crowley left the mortuary and walked into the sun filled afternoon. He was shocked to find the day so pleasant. He squinted, knowing exactly what the doc had meant about the visor. He smiled in spite of the trouble that murder brought.

The Chief stopped on the way back to the office for something to eat from the hot dog stand on the corner of Lopes Square. Mike Moone was behind the counter. "I hear there's a dead guy out at Richland's," Mike said.

Crowley was on guard. "There's always a dead guy at Richland's. It's what he does. But since your asking, yes. Mr. Alves, remember him. Ninety-two years old. Nice man. He lived a good long life." Crowley picked up the hot dogs and walked straight to the squad car.

Chapter 3

The Chief was at his desk making notes on index cards for the corkboard when Dr. Rice came in.

"James, I'm getting too old for this." The doctor's wide frame overflowed the sides of the chair as he eased himself in. A year ago the doctor told Crowley that he was hoping to retire, but it seemed there was always one more patient, one more birth, and now one more murder.

"You look tired, doc," the chief said. The doctor's eyelids drooped and he looked like he could fall asleep right there.

"Just a little worn down at the edges. Death has a way of making me feel ninety years old." Then the doctor took a serious tone and began a verbal report. "I'd say the man is approximately thirty years old. He was five-foot ten-inches and weighted approximately one hundred-seventy pounds. Except for the fact that he's dead, he looked to be in good physical condition. The medical examiner will tell you more." Doctor Rice continued, "You saw the wound. I don't have a match on the weapon, yet. Now you know as much as I do. Any questions?"

"Did you fingerprint him?" the chief asked.

"Yes, of course, this isn't my first murder case, as you very well know." The doctor reached into the black bag that he always carried and produced two slips of paper. "Here's a copy of his prints. His fingers were swollen and not in great condition. I did what I could."

He handed the papers to the chief and continued, "And two copies of the death certificate, one for you and the other for the County Medical Examiner. Both are made out for John Doe." He closed his medical bag. "I'm too old for this, or did I already say that."

The doctor grunted as he moved in the chair. He chuckled and then continued. "I also took a couple of pictures using my latest gadget, a new Kodak Super Six camera. It's a beauty, expensive but worth it. I'll develop the photos myself and have them for you in a couple of days." The doctor had taken up the hobby and had a variety of cameras and developing equipment in his basement.

The weary doctor continued, "I spoke to the State Medical Examiner. They'll pick up the body. So if you think you need another look at the man before they take him, it'll have to be soon. You know where to find me." Rice put his hands down on his thighs and pushed himself up. While picking up his black bag he looked Crowley in the eyes. "I'll keep looking for that instrument of death." He said the last three words using an accent like that of Bela Lugosi as Count Dracula in the movies.

Crowley laughed. "Very funny. You're not getting too old for this," the chief said. "All you need is a good hot meal and a hug from that great lady you're married to." The chief rose and the men shook hands.

"And a good night's sleep wouldn't hurt either," Dr. Rice added. "Call me if you have any brilliant ideas or if another body washes up."

Crowley walked the doctor out. After Dr. Rice departed he turned to Lewis. "Did you find a chart?" Lewis answered in the affirmative. Crowley continued, "Good. Bring a couple of cups of your best coffee. Thanks."

Lewis came in carrying a tray containing the steaming cups and a book with a yellow cover. He also had a three-foot long chart rolled up, tucked under his arm. "I called the Steel Pier Company," Lewis said. "They gave me a schedule of both arriving and departing. The fellow said that as far as he knew all their employees were accounted for and no passengers reported missing."

Lewis set the tray on the desk and handed the chief a copy of

Eldridge's Tide Book. "The high and low tides are listed by month," he told the chief. A tab of paper was sticking out from the top of the book, marking the month of June.

The patrolman added, "Did you know that George Eldridge of Chatham was the originator of the tide book? He moved to Martha's Vineyard with his son, also named George by the way. The son began selling the book to vessels that anchored outside Vineyard Haven Harbor, waiting for a fair tide in Nantucket Sound. Young George would sail out to meet them in his catboat and sell them his father's book. It was very successful. The son published the first tide book in 1875 that contained the tides for places other than Nantucket Sound. And now everyone who travels by water knows his name." Lewis's face seemed to light up. His smile made creases in his cheeks that lifted his ears.

The chief chuckled, "You're a font of information Lewis. Now let's get back to work."

They unrolled the chart of Cape Cod Bay. It showed the depths of the bottom, the curvature of the sea floor, and listed latitude and longitude from Boston to Long Point. He spread the three-foot square paper across the chief's desk and anchored it with the coffee mugs. They leaned over the map. Lewis opened the tide book. "Yesterday's high tide was at eight-thirty pm, low at two-thirty am, give or take a few minutes." Lewis made a sweeping motion with his index finger in a counter clockwise movement around the chart showing the direction of the incoming tide.

The two officers spent two hours talking about the possibilities: where the man entered the water, what was the weapon, and why did the body have to wash up in their town. "With the flow of water coming in every twelve hours, the body could have started anywhere. The water would take it out and bring it back." The two men looked at each other and then at the chart.

The chief continued, "Doc said the man was dead at least twenty-four hours. The tide would have gone out, come in, gone out and in again. Right?" The two men stopped to do the math. "It takes approximately six hours for the tide to come in and six to go out. Today is Thursday. Of coarse it's a guess, but I'd say the time of death was Tuesday maybe as far back as Monday. The coroner will give us a better idea." The chief sat down at his desk chair and put his hands behind his neck as if trying to hold up his head. He looked at the ceiling.

"I need some fresh air." The chief picked up his hat and headed for the door. "Stay at the front desk, Lewis. I'll be back soon," he said.

Lewis replied that he'd brought a sandwich from home and could stay as long as the chief needed him.

Crowley drove east on Bradford Street until he came to the intersection of Commercial where the two streets then became County Road. Houses gave way to thick woods. A half-mile further along was the east-end breakwater. He pulled the Chevy onto the dirt shoulder, got out, and began walking alongside the road. The expanse of Cape Cod Bay was on his right. This was the edge of his town. He often drove here, looked out across the bay and then turned around to drive slowly back observing the houses, tightly packed along the front street, filled now with summer people.

He walked along the edge of the road. The ground in front of him was a mix of sand, rock and pavement. There were a few cigarette butts, some shards of broken glass, rusted pieces of metal, a smattering of wood, rocks of all sizes, but nothing of consequence.

Marks in the dirt at the edge of the pavement caught his attention. Crowley was drawn to the treads that were imprinted in the soft sand on the shoulder of the road. Right now they were discernable, but he knew wind or rain would eradicate them. He bent down and touched the impression. The front and rear wheels on the right side of a vehicle had left the pavement.

"How many vehicles had pulled over at this particular spot

in the past couple of days," he wondered. "Tourists to look at the view, someone needing to turn around, lovers or friends stopping to talk, or perhaps a stop for a more sinister reason?"

The imprint had a zigzag pattern. He took his notebook from his shirt pocket and made a rough drawing of what he was looking at. It might prove useful, most likely ineffectual, but you never knew. He kept a notebook filled with all kinds of information. After surveying the view he headed back to the center of town.

Chapter 4

The following morning Chief James Crowley was having a cup of coffee while berating himself that a day had passed without identifying John Doe. No report had come in of missing fisherman or a missing loved one. He found that perplexing. His office was silent. Crowley spent the next hour looking over the notes, scratching off names and jotting down ideas that led nowhere. The tide chart had been helpful but didn't prove anything. He felt like a penned dog ready to burst out. He didn't like the idea that he had no leads.

The town was quiet at this early hour. The fishermen had already departed and the tourists had yet to appear on the streets. Most shops were still closed. The body had been placed in a tomb at the town cemetery. Unidentified remains, a body waiting for internment when the ground was frozen, or victims of suspicious death were kept in the crypt. This time the corpse was placed in the town's vault because Mr. Richland didn't have refrigeration and the corpse could not be embalmed until after the Barnstable County Medical Examiner's Office did the mandated autopsy.

Crowley heard the front door open and Lewis called back to him. "Should I bring coffee?"

Instead of answering Crowley walked the hallway to the counter where Lewis was moving around behind his desk. "No coffee, thanks. I ate at Betty's." The chief was restless, tapped his fingers on the counter top. "Why hasn't anyone reported this man as missing? It's unbelievable that no one is looking for him," Crowley said to Lewis.

"He's definitely not from town," Lewis replied. "We would have heard something by now."

"All the same, get on the phone to the various fish buyers in town. I know there are twenty-five, so it will take you most of the morning. See if they've heard anything about a missing person. When you finish that start calling around to the harbormasters on the cape." Lewis nodded and the chief continued, "I'll call Detective Shiff in Boston later this morning. Let's broaden our search."

Crowley stopped for a moment wondering if there was something else he should be doing. "Right now I'm going to take a ride through town, check the heartbeat and I want to have another look at the east end breakwater. I won't be long."

The chief was putting off the inevitable. Shiff was a good man. Crowley liked the guy. He was the detective with the experience and contacts. And Crowley had to agree that Shiff made things happen. But Crowley couldn't shake the feeling that the Boston Detective was judging him.

He reminded the chief of his father who would give him difficult tasks, from stacking a cord of wood when he was seven years old, to writing thank you notes to the ladies from the church for their help at the holidays, and everything had to be perfect. His father would watch the progress without giving help or hints to how he was doing. James was never given money or reward for the work he did at home. It was expected.

Crowley cleared his mind as he walked for a second time along County Road. The breakwater's grey boulders, covered in lichen, ragged, and spiritless were almost entirely covered by water. The wind had taken care of the tire tracks. Looking back toward town he noticed the side of Mrs. Alter's house. It glowed in the distance from the sun's reflection, pearly white with black shutters. There was a question he'd like to ask her. He knew he could call, but it would only take a minute to stop on his way back to the office.

A woman, not Sara Alter, opened the door when he knocked. Her dark chestnut hair was wet and hung in ringlets to her shoulders. Crowley looked into grey-green eyes and was unable to speak, a rarity for him.

"Can I help you?" She asked. Her dress was soft blue with white polka dots and her feet were bare. She held a towel over her arm. "If your looking for my aunt, she's gone into town. I expect her back at any moment."

He cleared his throat and said, "Yes, thank you. I'm James Crowley, the Provincetown Police Chief." There was something familiar about her. "I'm sorry if I've disturbed your shower."

She laughed. "Not a shower, I've just come from a swim. I know who you are." She invited him in. "My aunt will be back in a few minutes. Have a seat. Can I get you a glass of water?"

His nodded yes, his throat suddenly felt dry.

Seagulls swooped and cried. Waves sloshed against the deck, but Crowley hardly noticed. He was looking at the woman walking toward him with a glass in each hand. It had been a while since he'd had female company. Eleanor, his high school sweetheart married his best friend while he was in the Army. He had dated a few local women, but they left him deflated and depressed. He had sworn off romantic ties after the last lady had made him nervous with talk of marriage. But now he was looking at this woman with renewed interest.

"Do I know you?" Crowley asked as she handed him the water.

She smiled, sat in the chair opposite, and then laughed. "You wouldn't remember me. I was a freshman when you were a senior. My name is Susan Jahnig. I lived in Provincetown during my high school years." She gave him a brief description of where she went after graduation. "I didn't grow up here. We moved back to the city right after graduation."

She took a sip of water and continued, "I now teach school and have the summer off. When Aunt Sara invited me to spend the summer. I jumped at the chance."

They talked for half an hour before the front door opened. "I see you two have met. What brings you here, Chief?" Mrs. Alter's eyes jumped between the two like watching a tennis match. Crowley stood up. They both looked guilty, of what no one knew.

Chief Crowley straightened his shoulders and said, "I wanted to ask you if you can see the breakwater from your deck?" She looked at the chief then looked out toward the water.

Crowley continued speaking as they walked toward the glass French doors that led to the porch. "Did you happen to see any cars or trucks stop at the breakwater, maybe Monday or Tuesday night?" Chief Crowley knew he was grasping at straws. "I was just wondering if maybe you had noticed anything unusual."

"Well yes." She opened the door. Squinting her eyes, looking to the left at the rocks in the distance she added, "I can see the breakwater, but no, I don't remember seeing any cars stopping there. I don't recall anything unusual. Occasionally a vehicle will stop. It's the view. You can see the whole town from there. Cars and trucks come and go from town, but it's usually quiet at night."

Mrs. Alter went back inside and took her niece's arm as if holding it for reassurance. She smiled at the chief. "I've tried to put that dreadful episode out of my mind. My niece arrived last evening and I'm so glad she's here. I told her all about the body on the beach. I hope that was alright?" Mrs. Alter waited for him to speak. His eyes lingered on her niece.

He said, "Yes, that's fine. Well I thought I would stop to see how you are doing. Thank you, Mrs. Alter. If you remember anything from that night, please give me a call." He wrote his name and phone numbers, the station and home, on a piece of paper that he tore from his note pad.

She nodded and asked Susan to see the chief to the door. They paused at the sill. "It was good to see you again after all these years," the chief said. "Perhaps we could talk again. May I call you?" She smiled and said that would be nice.

Slipping into the police car he began whistling a tune that he'd heard on the radio sung by Ella Fitzgerald, *A Tisket, a Tasket, A Red and Yellow Basket.* The visit didn't help his investigation at all, but he was sure glad he'd decided to stop.

Chapter 5

Back at the station he thanked Lewis for holding down the fort. "I'll be in my office." Crowley was still humming the tune when he picked up the phone. He dialed 0. The rotary disc clicked off ten digits. He gave the operator a Boston phone number.

The police department switchboard put him through to a voice he recognized. "Shiff." Crowley pictured the detective sitting in his office with a cigarette in one hand and the phone in the other. Balding, potbellied and short, the man spoke with rapid staccato words. He gave orders like he owned the place, wherever he was.

"Hello, Charlie. This is James Crowley. Are you still keeping the peace up there in Boston?" Crowley liked the gruff, fast talking detective.

"There's not a whisper of crime when I'm on the job, you know that." He chuckled. "To what do I owe the honor of a call from the tip of Cape Cod?"

Crowley reported what he knew about the body on the beach, giving Shiff the few sketchy details. "I was hoping that maybe you could check with Boston's missing persons for us. See if anyone answering his description has been reported AWOL in the metropolitan area. I'll send a picture of the man, although he's not looking too good. Doc Rice took his photograph post-mortem."

Crowley hesitated, unsure how to proceed. "I wouldn't ask but it seems we are at a standstill. We have no reports of missing persons on this end. It's my feeling that the victim isn't from this area." Communications between the many police departments had been expanding and cooperation was improving. Unlikely friendships had formed. "And perhaps if I sent you a copy of his fingerprints you could do some comparing." Crowley wondered if he was pushing it. "Could be a felon and perhaps you have a record of him."

"Sure," the Boston Detective said, stretching the word making it sound longer than it actual was. "It's not like I have anything else to do." Both men knew sarcasm when they heard it. The detective continued, "Look, you know as well as I do that fingerprint comparison is very time consuming and chances are slim to none that we'll get a match. It could take weeks, maybe months to find a match." Crowley imagined experts sitting with magnifying glasses looking at swirls and patterns trying to find one that closely fit. "It's a million to one chance," Shiff said.

Crowley tried to interrupt, "Ok, okay, I get it."

The Boston Detective ignored him and kept talking, "Everyday we have reports of missing persons. Listen, I'll have copies made of the photo and send them along with his vitals to the various precinct stations around Boston. I'll get the picture out, but don't hold your breath. It could take awhile." Crowley heard a cigarette being inhaled.

Shiff continued, "If we get any results, that's a big if, I'll let you know." Shiff had a habit of talking fast. The only thing that slowed him down was inhaling nicotine. He liked to get his thoughts out quickly and then move on.

"On another note, I have some news that I'm about to share with all the Cape Cod Police Departments. While I have you on the phone, I'll fill you in."

Detective Shiff was Boston's liaison to the FBI's newly formed Committee Investigating Un-American Activities. This committee was created in 1938 by the House of Representatives to investigate alleged disloyalty and subversive activities with particular interest in organizations suspected of having Nazi, Fascist, or Communist ties.

Shiff took the Provincetown Police Chief by surprise. "I've had word that a group of Nazi sympathizers has formed somewhere on the cape. The Bureau has asked us to keep our eyes and ears open. Wherever they show up it means trouble."

Shiff explained, "We're not sure where the meetings are being held. Most likely they move around, trying not to draw too much attention to their group." The Boston police officer paused to inhale. "Mark my words, we'll be drawn into a war with Germany. It's a mess over there."

News was filtering in from across Europe. Shiff continued, "Russia has signed a non-intervention pact with Germany. It means no interference while Hitler annexes Poland." Everyone knew that England and France had declared war on Germany and Italy had invaded Ethiopia. Political unrest was at an all time high. War was rapidly spreading across Europe.

"To make matters worse, right here in America a radical fringe element is preaching German supremacy and touting that a superior race is needed. Hate mongers filling needy people with their evil." Detective Shiff's voice was raised an octave. He had strong convictions. He told Crowley that America should not wait, but send aid and supplies to England. "Now before it's too late."

Crowley had seen first hand the devastation of the Great War. In 1919 he was an eighteen-year old Army private whose job it was to help with what was called mopping up. It had been a task that left a mark on him.

Shiff and Crowley had talked before about these same issues. Unfortunately, the news of war was getting worse. Many Americans still hoped that America would remain neutral. President Franklin Roosevelt in his weekly radio address assured American citizens that he and his cabinet were doing everything they could to protect our great nation. It was Roosevelt's utmost wish to keep the country out of war, but young men everywhere were signing up to support Uncle Sam should the country be pulled into the conflict.

Crowley replied into the phone. "If I hear anything about

suspicious doings in Provincetown you'll be the first one I'll call. This is a small community, not much goes on here that we don't find out about. Thanks for helping with my problem." The two police officers said their goodbyes, each hoping that neither murder nor war would settle on their doorsteps. Crowley leaned back in his chair, thinking about Nazis, war, and murder.

James Crowley had enlisted in the Army and was trained as Military Police. In the aftermath of WWII his job was to help with relocating and reuniting families. The war was over when he was in Europe, but he had witnessed the results. It left him with strong feelings about war. The horror of what had taken place in the trenches was felt in the hearts of men and women across the world.

Crowley returned to the states. He went to the University of Massachusetts and after graduating, to the Police Academy. He worked in New Bedford for a few years before returning to his native Provincetown as Police Chief.

A knock on the chief's open door brought Lewis into the office. "Is there anything I can do for you before I head home?" he asked.

"Well, there is one thing I'd like to ask." It had slipped the chief's mind. "Do you think you could stop at Richland's Funeral Home and give condolences to the Alves family from the department? Since you're already in uniform just stop and show your face, or in this case the uniform. Our department needs representation. I'll give you extra time off when you need it." It was an arrangement they had used before and it worked for both men.

It only took a minute for Lewis to say that he would. "I'll just call home and tell Ma. Maybe she'll want to go with me. I'll ask. Two birds with one stone, so to speak."

Crowley thanked the patrolman. "I'll be here a while longer. Can you use your mother's car to go out to Richland's or would you like to take the squad car?"

"I'll take my mom's, thanks," the patrolman answered.

If the chief didn't have an unsolved murder case sitting on his desk he would have gone, even though he didn't know Mr. Alves. It was a matter of respect. "I wish I could give you a raise, Lewis," the chief said.

The patrolman left and the chief thought about the young officer. Not many people knew that his name was Lewis A Lewis. The chief smiled and went back to reading his notes and writing on index cards.

Chapter 6

Crowley had the doctor's report in front of him and was reading it for what seemed like the hundredth time when the phone rang. "Provincetown Police Department, Chief Crowley speaking."

The woman on the other end identified herself as Helen Garrison. "I live at number 49 Bradford Street near Nickerson. I want to know if someone can park a car in front of your house and leave it there. My son is coming with his wife and family and they always park in front of my house." Her voice grew louder when she said the last two words. She waited for the chief to speak.

Crowley hesitated, thinking about the reply. "Mam, I don't believe it is against the law to park a car overnight or for a few days. And I don't believe I can have it removed." The chief was certain that there was no rule on the books that dealt with cars parked on the street. "I can have a look, maybe get in touch with the owner."

He didn't want to upset the old woman, but he had to let her know what the law could and could not do. "I can't force the person to move it and I don't think I can give him or her a ticket either," he said, "But I'll look into it."

"Well, find out whose car it is and ask him to move it by Friday morning. Tell them they can put it back next Monday. The family is only staying the weekend." It sounded like an order. Helen Garrison hung up without saying goodbye.

The chief planned to pick up a few groceries on the way home and he wanted to restock his supply of Whiskey so he decided to add another stop on his route. Maybe he could placate Mrs. Garrison.

With tourist season rapidly approaching and so many people bringing their automobiles with them, the idea of new regulations governing parking, traffic patterns, and speed limits needed to be addressed by the town's selectmen. The chief would write up some suggestions and present them at their weekly meeting. He'd have to wear his uniform. Just the thought of it made him scratch his neck as he drove west on Bradford Street.

The Police Chief stopped the squad car across the street from Helen Garrison's house. A black four-door Oldsmobile was parked there, blocking the path to the house. Mrs. Garrison lived in a cape style house that was in need of paint. Wooden stairs led to a brick walkway. The path went directly to the street and stopped at the automobile. Crowley was looking at the car when the front door opened.

Mrs. Garrison might be in her eighties, but she was not frail. She walked with a sure step. An apron covered most of the front of her housedress and her heavy black shoes clapped against the wood as she made her way toward the chief. She held onto a walking stick. The yard had no fence. Weeds grew a foot high on both sides of the path. There was a neglected feel about the place that sometimes happens when old ladies live alone.

"Hi chief," she hollered. "You'll have to speak up." She put her hand up to her ear. "I was hoping you could ask the owner to park it somewhere else. It would be nice if my son could park their automobile in front of our house."

"Mrs. Garrison." The chief tipped the brim of his hat and then spoke with a raised voice. "Mam, like I said on the phone, I can't legally force the owner to move it, but I can find out who owns this fine car and have a word with him or her." The chief removed his notepad from his shirt pocket and wrote down the plate number, the year and make of the car. "How long has it been parked there?" The chief called over his shoulder.

The old woman squinted her eyes together as if looking for clarity. "If I remember correctly, it was a couple of days ago, around eight o'clock in the evening. I think it was, but with the June days being so long it might have been a little later. I was just turning on the light in the living room, that's how I come to see him. I think it was Tuesday because I remember thinking my family wouldn't be here till Saturday, so there was no need to bother the man about parking. My memory isn't what it used to be, could have been Monday." The woman was sharper than the chief expected and glad of it. "I expect he's staying somewhere in the neighborhood."

The chief peeked in the windows and then took hold of the handle. It was unlocked. Opening the driver's side door, he had a feeling that he was trespassing, but he excused this by thinking that the car might be stolen or abandoned. Of coarse he knew it was ridiculous to think anyone would just leave such a fine automobile. The owner would be back.

There was a cardboard box on the front seat, passenger side. The lid was open. Crowley peeked in. There were pamphlets, printed in both English and what looked to him to be German. A large swastika was stamped at the top of the paper. The chief didn't read what was written. The hair on his arms stood up. "Well, well, look what we have here?" He took one of the sheets of paper, folded it, and tucked it into his pocket.

Closing the door, he turned to Helen Garrison. "We'll have to leave the car here for the time being, but I'll see what can be done. Sorry about the inconvenience to you and your family. I'm sure it won't be long before this vehicle is moved."

Helen thanked the chief for coming and said, "I know he can park on the street, but I am hoping the fellow will be kind enough move the car before my family gets here. My daughter-in-law has trouble walking, Rheumatoid Arthritis."

The policeman nodded, and then asked, "Did you happen to see the man who parked the car here?"

"I didn't get a good look. It was getting dark. He was medium build, a little shorter than you. He was a white man, not dark Portuguese. I'm not sure about his hair color."

Crowley asked, "Did you see which way he went?"

She stopped for a moment, tapped her index finger on her chin, and shook her head. "Sorry, I saw him get out of the car. I didn't pay too much attention. There are no rooming houses up this end of town, so I thought maybe he was visiting family or friends." That was all Helen Garrison could tell the policeman.

Houses lined both sides of Bradford Street in both directions. Crowley knew the person who owned the car could be in any of the neighboring houses. Crowley wrote a few lines in his notebook. He was now anxious to get back to the station and call the Motor Vehicle Registry as well as his friend Shiff.

"Thank you Mrs. Garrison. I'll see what I can do. Have a nice visit with your family, " the chief said. He got into the patrol car, did a U-turn on Bradford Street and headed back to the center of town.

Chapter 7

Crowley unlocked the police station door. He left his groceries in the car but brought the bottle of whiskey in with him. He switched on the light and went straight to the desk behind the counter where Lewis always sat. The chief opened the top drawer and took the list of important phone numbers that Lewis kept there into his office.

He placed the unopened bottle on the desk and picked up the phone. The operator asked the chief what number he wanted. He gave her the Hyannis number and said he wished to be connected to the Registry of Motor Vehicles.

"That office closes at five pm, sir," the operator said. "You'll have to call back tomorrow."

Crowley muttered under his breath. "This is Police Chief James Crowley. Isn't there anyone there that can help me?" He asked.

The operator was polite, "Sorry Chief, everyone's gone. It's closed."

Chief Crowley looked at the clock on the wall, realizing he's lost track of time. He thanked her and hung up. After a few minutes of tugging on his mustache he took the phone out of its cradle.

For the second time that day he called Detective Shiff. An operator at the Boston Police Department switchboard picked up the call. The chief gave her his name and asked to be put through to Detective Charles Shiff. "One moment sir," she said. The phone on the other end rang six times while Crowley waited. The switchboard operator broke in, "I'm sorry sir, he doesn't answer. Can I take a message? I'll see that he gets it."

Chief Crowley spelled his name and gave her his home phone number. "Tell him it's important," the chief added.

There was nothing more he could do. The registry was closed and Shiff unavailable. He looked at the bottle of scotch, picked it up, and poured himself a shot. He drank it in one swallow, set the bottle in the bottom left drawer, picked up his hat and headed for home. Crowley drove west on Bradford Street instead of his usual route along Commercial Street. The car was still parked in front of Mrs. Garrison's house.

He pulled over to the side and stared at the vehicle as if it held some secret that he had yet to discover. He thought about the implications of what he'd seen and what he'd been told by Mrs. Garrison. There was a light on in the front room of her home, but he didn't see any movement. The chief sat in the patrol car, waiting without purpose, hoping someone would show up. No one did. He had a vague feeling that the owner of the vehicle wouldn't be coming back anytime soon. He headed home.

Crowley carried the *Advocate* into the living room after eating and sat in his favorite chair. He opened the newspaper. The front-page story was about the town's fishermen. A group had gone to Boston to request that the State give relief to the fishermen who would not be able to use their nets after dark within three miles of the coast if a certain bill passed. The bill had been defeated and the fishermen were assured that night fishing inside three miles could continue.

The president of the Provincetown Fishermen's Association was quoted as saying "The forty draggers in Provincetown are the only means of livelihood for 1500 people and provide work indirectly for hundreds of others in industries closely connected with fishing."

The article described the meeting with the Governor's Commission, the Provincetown fishermen, and State Representative E. Hayes Small of Truro who chaired the meeting.

Crowley knew these men who fished for a living. He pictured them sitting down with the governor. The thought made him chuckle.

Chief Crowley admired the men and their efforts. Fishing was the heart of Provincetown. Fishermen spent their money in town. They stimulated the economy with the purchase of groceries, boots, rope, iron hooks, wooden boxes, wire, spools of twine, fids, sailcloth, fuel, engine parts, baskets, insurance, mortgages, and many other items too numerous to count. And that didn't include the tourists who came to Provincetown for a fresh fish dinner.

They provide food. They share with the community, provide free fish to those in need, and give heavily to charity. Just yesterday Captain Billy Adams came into the station to talk about the fishermen holding a fish fry and another dance at the Town Hall.

Crowley watched Billy swagger into the office. Adams was the youngest captain in the fleet and some would say a bit cocky. He had dark eyes that crinkled at the edge forming upturned creases when he smiled. His skin, weathered from sun and wind, resembled soft leather.

Adams told the chief about the Fishermen's Association's plans. "They are asking if you would support the fish fry and the dance. Would you speak in favor to the Board of Selectmen?"

The chief nodded, "I have no problem with the men holding functions. From what I understand the last dance was a great success." Crowley said he'd be glad to address the selectmen and that he would come to the next fishermen's association meeting to hear the details.

"The fishermen will be donating the profits to the churches this year, St. Peter's, St. Mary's, the Methodists, and the Universalists. We're trying to cover all our bases." The fisherman gave a nod of his head and was about to leave when the chief stopped him.

Crowley asked, "How's the fishing?"

"Slow," the captain said. "June always is. The fish are moving and the lobsters are taking over. I'm thinking of going for sea clams. There's not much money in clams, but I have to do something." The captain didn't say more. He seemed in a hurry. Adams thanked the chief, tipped his fishermen's cap, and left.

Thinking about the dance caused the chief to remember the first Anniversary Ball. That was an awful night. It took a team effort to stop a murderer. Crowley's body shook as he remembered how close they came to losing Mary Diogo, his godchild. And that reminded him that he hadn't seen her parents, Manny and Eleanor, in a few weeks. He made a note to stop by and tell Manny about the dance. The chief didn't think that the shopkeeper would be interested in volunteering for this event, not after what he'd gone through during the last one, but you never know how men will react.

He was thinking about the Anniversary Ball when the phone rang. He picked up and said, "Crowley here."

"I got your message. What's up? The switchboard said it was important," the Boston detective said.

"Hold on a minute please," Crowley said, "I'm waiting for the telephone operator to hang up on her end. Do you hear me Tillie?" There was a click as the operator disconnected. Crowley continued, "Telephone operators are the biggest source of gossip in this town. I'd like this conversation to stay between the two of us." He waited to be sure no one else was on the line.

Silence filled the air until the chief spoke. "Not only do I have some information on the Party you were talking about, but I think we may have a lead on my victim. They may be linked." The chief described the automobile, what was inside, and how Mrs. Garrison had described the man that left the car on Tuesday night.

"I called the registry, but they were closed. I'll have the name and address of the owner tomorrow morning. If it turns out that the owner is alive and well, then you have information to give to your friends at the FBI. And I'll keep trying to identify John Doe."

Crowley knew that this tip would put both the Boston PD and the federal agencies on alert.

"I can't see why a man would leave an expensive car like that and not come back to move it or check on it. I have a feeling we have someone in common."

Charles Shiff didn't hesitate. "Interesting. Sounds promising. I have to make some arrangements, but I'll be coming to Provincetown. And I'm bringing someone with me, one of my best. Have the vehicle watched. We'll talk tomorrow." The chief bristled at being given orders by the Boston detective, but said nothing.

Shiff's words sounded like rapid gunfire, each pronounced with emphasis. The chief could tell that Shiff was excited when he added, "We'll need more, but this is getting interesting, yes indeed."

Before the two policemen said goodnight, Crowley mentioned the dance the fishermen were planning, a second anniversary ball. "Good, maybe this time you'll get to dance with the girl of your dreams," Shiff said and then hung up.

Chapter 8

James Crowley was up before the sun. The day would be beautiful, warm, dry, and with just enough breeze to make it memorable. He was out the door and on the way to Betty's Luncheonette before the sun hit the horizon. First he checked on the automobile. It had not moved.

After breakfast he checked the Oldsmobile again. It was still in front of Helen Garrisons' home. He drove slowly up the hill toward the meadowlands, looking at the homes, the cross streets, the area. He made a U-turn at the top of the hill and was at his desk reading through his notes when Lewis came in.

"You're in early, chief. Has something happened?" Lewis came to work at eight o'clock every day, five days a week and did whatever the chief asked. Lewis was thoughtful, quiet, and knew the town's people and its history. He talked to everyone as he made his rounds through the town's center. Crowley was grateful for his loyalty.

Crowley did not keep a schedule because he put in more time than required. He answered calls at all hours. The town was small enough for him to be at the caller's house in less than ten minutes. The month of June had been unusually quiet. Crime was minimal, if you didn't count the murder.

At their morning meeting Lewis and Crowley talked about Mrs. Garrison and the car on Bradford Street. "I'd like you to take the squad car and park where you can keep an eye on it. Don't disturb it, stay far enough away and try not to attract attention. Just watch. If anyone comes for it, call me on the car's radio."

The phone on the desk rang. Crowley grabbed the receiver. He said yes a few times, wrote on a piece of paper, and then thanked the person on the other end. When he hung up, he saw that Lewis was waiting with eyes wide.

"Well," the chief said, "That was the Registry of Motor Vehicles. The owner of the car doesn't live in Provincetown. His name is Frank White. He lives in Gloucester. I have an address. I'll call the chief of police up there. Let's see what he can tell us about the abandoned car." He took the keys to the squad car from his desktop and handed them to Lewis.

Lewis jiggled the keys. "Then I'll get myself up to the west end and stay near that car till I hear from you. I'll keep the radio on channel sixteen and my eyes on the Oldsmobile."

The chief knew that his sergeant would do as he was told. "Call me on the radio if it moves. If someone comes for it, don't let it out of your sight."

After Lewis left, Crowley picked up the phone and asked Tillie to get the Gloucester Police Department. "I'd like to speak to the chief of police." His call went through another switchboard, and then a series of secretaries before Crowley was routed to the man in charge.

"This is Chief O'Malley. How can I help you," the man on the other end said.

"This is Police Chief James Crowley from Provincetown. I was wondering if I could get your help."

After listening to the situation, O'Malley said he would have one of his patrolmen go to the address. "We'll ask a few questions and hopefully be able to give you some answers by this afternoon." Chief O'Malley was friendly, courteous, got right to the point, and was careful about any prediction of outcome.

The next phone call was to Shiff. He let the Boston Detective know what he had learned. Both men had an interest in the vehicle.

Lewis spent the day sitting in the squad car waiting for something to happen. He ate a sandwich and drank a bottle of Moxie. He watched the traffic on Bradford Street. A few trucks drove past, as did cars with people he recognized, cars with persons he didn't know, and two horses with riders who came up toward him from the other side of the hill. A group of people walked past, carrying sacs, heading toward the beach at the end of Bradford Street. The day was quiet.

At three o'clock in the afternoon a man tapped on the window and said, "Chief Crowley sent me." The man showed Lewis his badge. "Harry Enos is the name."

Enos wore street clothing and Lewis thought he looked like a plumber in coveralls. He had a jacket flung over his shoulder. "I'm with the State Police, undercover. I'll take over from here. You can go."

Lewis told his replacement that no one had come near the car. The man nodded, but didn't say anything more. He crossed the street and got into an unmarked 1933 Ford Coupe. Lewis watched Enos get into the black vehicle. He thought he saw a bulge beneath the undercover policeman's cotton shirt as he reached to open the car door. It was the Boston cop's turn to sit and watch.

Lewis headed straight back to the office. Crowley wasn't alone. The chief looked up and said, "Lewis, you remember Detective Shiff?" It was not a question, Shiff was known to them. Shiff stood and shook Lewis's hand.

"I met your man, Enos." Lewis nodded at the Boston Detective. "No one has come near the car all day." Looking at Crowley, he continued, "If you want I can go back in the morning." His eyes caught the swastika at the top of the paper lying on the chief's desk.

Crowley opened his mouth to speak, but was interrupted by the Boston policeman. "No, no that's all right. Let's keep my man on watch. The owner is bound to show up to take the car eventually. If he turns out to be your victim, well that's another matter. Could be just a coincidence that the car appeared at the same time as your John Doe."

Shiff was right, but Crowley didn't believe in coincidence. He listened and nodded his head. Detective Shiff continued. "You never know, maybe you'll get a match. I don't want to jump the gun here, so let's be patient. James, I'm hoping someone shows up for that car. If it moves we'll follow." The two policemen had the same ideas, just different priorities.

"The owner may not have anything to do with the man on the beach. I'm sure we'd all like to get a handle on this Nazi group, maybe crack it open like a barrel of monkeys." Shiff laughed at his own joke.

"If he turns out to be my victim," Crowley hesitated, "I'll have the car impounded and go over it with a fine-toothed comb. I'll find out where he works, who he hangs out with, and who his family is. If the murderer is in my town, he won't get away with it." The chief's voice was firm.

The room grew silent. The phone rang. The chief picked it up, identified himself, and listened. He took a pencil and made notes as he said things like, "Go ahead. Yes. Yes. OK. Could you repeat that? Yes. I understand. Thank you. I'll be in touch." He placed the phone back into the cradle and tapped the pencil on his notepad. Both Lewis and Shiff looked at the Chief.

"That was Gloucester PD. The owner of the vehicle, Frank White, lives at that address. They met his landlady. She said he lives alone, hasn't been back to his room in about a week, which she said was not unusual seeing how he's a traveling salesman."

Crowley took a deep breath. "The landlady said he comes and goes. He drives an Oldsmobile. She didn't know what year. His rent is paid for the month." Crowley stopped speaking and looked at Shiff.

"Let's get a photograph of our John Doe up to the landlady and see if she can ID him. Crowley paused as if not wanting to verbalize his thoughts. "He may not be our victim, but by this time tomorrow we'll know one way or another." The men sat in the small office space without saying anything. They could hear the clock on the wall telling them that they needed to keep moving in a timely fashion.

"I can make the run to Gloucester. It's closer to Boston. It would take you all day to get there and back," Shiff said.

The Boston detective rubbed the stubble on his chin. "I'll speak to the landlady. If she can identify him from that picture your doctor took, then you have a match." He looked at the chief, pulled a cigarette from his jacket pocket. He didn't light it, just held it in his hand.

Crowley pushed an ashtray across the desk. "Thanks, that'll save time."

Shiff was short and stocky, built like a wrestler or a prizefighter. His chest expanded as he lit the cigarette and drew in a breath. The Boston Detective continued, "And if not, well, I get to find out who Frank White is. Someone will come for the car eventually. But let's not get ahead of ourselves." The three men sat quietly, each with their own thoughts.

Shiff tapped his index finger on the piece of paper in front of Crowley. "I'd like to know where those pamphlets came from and where they were going," Shiff added. "I'll leave Enos on watch at the car. I'd better get going. I've got a superior who wants to know what I'm doing down here. I'll be in touch." Shiff crushed the cigarette into the ashtray. He left the office, leaving a trail of smoke behind him.

Chapter 9

True to his word, Detective Shiff left one of his best men in Provincetown. The Boston undercover cop sat watching the car in front of Mrs. Garrison's house. Just after midnight a man approached the Oldsmobile. Harry saw him open the door on the passenger side and take a cardboard box. The policeman waited. The man disappeared around the corner onto Nickerson Street. Then the officer slipped from his car and followed on foot at a safe distance. The stranger led him to a house at the end of the street.

Harry Enos watched the man enter through the front door. He noted the time, the number of the house, and a rough description of what he had observed. Back at his vehicle, he started the car and returned to town where he placed a call to his superior from a pay phone at the corner of Lopes Square.

At one o'clock in the morning the Provincetown Police Chief answered the ringing phone with a voice that sounded rough and groggy. "Crowley here," he said.

The other voice didn't waste time. "I'll be in Gloucester tomorrow morning. Better in the daylight anyway." Shiff took a breath and changed the subject. "Enos just called. We had movement at the car. Half-hour ago a man showed up at the Olds and took the box to 29 Nickerson Street." The Boston detective spoke in his usual rapid speech. "This is your town, your call, it's up to you."

Chief Crowley answered, "I'd rather wait and see if we get a match from the landlady."

The Boston policeman spoke softly as if he didn't want to wake anyone in his home. "I'll have Enos keep an eye on the fellow that took the box. He's waiting at a phone booth to hear from me."

They both knew, that no matter which way it turned out, it could only lead to bad places.

Crowley was sitting on the edge of the bed in the dark, his eyes wide open, and his mind whirling. "What did you say the address was?" Shiff gave it to him.

"I don't think I know who lives there, but it will be easy enough to find out." Crowley yawned as he spoke.

Shiff continued, "The fellow who took the box will be going to a meeting. I want to get a line on where those pamphlets are going. We'll bring him in for questioning eventually."

"As long as you don't lose him. This guy could be a murderer," Crowley said. Both men were silent. "I think it's too early to show our hand. We watch the man at 29 Nickerson," the chief said. "We'll have an ID tomorrow."

They agreed and said goodnight.

The morning was cloudy, the wind had picked up, and the day was already feeling damp. Crowley was at his desk well before seven. Lewis came in, set a percolator on the hot plate, and then went back to the chief's office. The patrolman unbuttoned his uniform jacket and sat facing the chief. "Feels like rain, a bit humid, maybe we'll have our first thunder storm of the season," Lewis said.

Crowley ignored the statement about weather and asked if Lewis knew who lived at 29 Nickerson Street? "It's the last house on the street," the chief said.

Lewis was quiet for a minute. "If my memory serves me right, that would be Mildred and Joe Kurtz. I'll check the town records to be sure. But I think they've lived in that house for a few years." The patrolman's head bobbed up and down.

He added, "She graduated from high school a few years ahead of me. Her maiden name is Sewall. You must have been in the Army at that time. Him, I don't know at all." The sergeant was a font of town gossip and information. "I'll call over to the assessors office, give me five minutes." Lewis was out the door and back in less time than that.

Crowley took advantage of the local knowledge whenever the need arose, but for some reason the chief didn't pay much attention to gossip. People told him things about his neighbors and fellow citizens, but unless it involved some illegal activity he didn't retain the busy talk. This time Crowley was listening.

"Yup, that's them, Joseph and Mildred Kurtz. She's pretty much a loner. He's a salesman of some sort. He's not from here, a walk-a-shore." Lewis used the term for one who comes by land. If he'd come by sea, he'd be a wash-a-shore.

Lewis continued, "You may have seen her around town, but she's not someone who sticks in your mind, if you know what I mean. She stays to herself. I don't think she goes out much, not social, if you know what I mean." Lewis went on to describe their house that backs up against the dunes at the end of Nickerson Street.

Crowley listened to the information. The patrolman lifted his shoulders, shook his head, and said, "That's about all I can tell you."

"Thanks Lewis. Boston PD has the house under surveillance. I want you to watch the car while we wait for the ID." Lewis got up to leave. "It won't be long."

"Let's find out as much as we can about Joe Kurtz and his wife. Meet me back here at ten o'clock. I'll have word from Gloucester by then. On your way back to the station I want you to go over to Town Hall and check at the Treasurer's Office. Find out if Kurtz owns the house, what he paid for it, the taxes, and anything else you can find out. Ask around the town hall, quietly, see if anyone knows him."

Lewis left the office as Chief Crowley began pulling on the edge of his mustache. He wrote in his notebook and then wrote the name Joe Kurtz on an index card.

Within the hour a call came through from Dr. Rice. "What can I help you with? I'm on my way out, so make it quick." The doctor was always busy.

Crowley got right to the point. "What can you tell me about Mr. and Mrs. Kurtz that live out on Nickerson?" The chief knew that beside the priest who wouldn't tell him anything, of all the people in town, the doctor was the one who would know the most about its citizens and there was no law that said the doctor couldn't help out the police.

Doctor Rice didn't hesitate, "Well, I know both her parents are dead, her maiden name is Sewall, and she is alone a great deal of the time. They have no children. She's only been in to see me a couple of times. I can check her records, but all I remember about her is that I set a broken arm a couple of years ago." The doctor stopped. Took a breath and continued.

"I don't know her husband at all. He's never been into my office. That's it. We can talk another time. Mrs. Williams is about to have her third child and it will most likely come quick." With that he hung up the phone. Crowley put the phone back into the cradle. He walked to the corkboard and stuck the card to it.

Chapter 10

The Provincetown Fishermen's Association held their meetings on Friday. Crowley was on his way to the Legion Hall with his hat pulled down tight and the collar on the slicker turned-up against the rain. A cool wind whipped the tenacious leaves of the Elm trees that lined Commercial Street causing a noise like that of someone unwrapping presents in tissue paper. It was a persistent rain, the kind that made the chief wish he was home sitting in his easy chair with a good book. It had been a busy day, but nothing had changed except the weather.

The stairs on the outside of the building were wet and slippery from the spring rain. Crowley entered a large room on the second floor. It was packed with men. Cigar and cigarette smoke hung in the air like the fog that can envelope the harbor. The windows were open, but gave little relief to the indoor clouds. His eyes felt irritated, from both the smoke and from lack of sleep.

A short bald man at the front of the room was talking about what the state representatives from the governor's committee had to say about easing restrictions on fishermen. An occasional cough broke the silence from the audience. In a clear voice the man said, "The State legislature listened and many spoke in our favor, but we will have to wait to see how the bill fares. The fight isn't over. Get everyone you can to write letters of support for the fishermen." Grunts and moans could be heard.

He banged the gavel, "Next on the agenda is the use of ice on the fish." The association President, Manual Dutra said that it had been suggested by the Acushnet Fish Company that we should add more ice to the fish during the summer months.

A low murmur took over the room. The president banged his gavel. He continued, "We could take a penny from every pound of fish sold. The money will remain with our Association. We can use it to buy ice as well as for conducting business. And we could use some of our association funds to advertise our product. Id like to get some opinions on this from you men," Manual said. "We need one voice when our decision is made."

Crowley listened to the reactions from the men. Big John stood up. "I've been fishing for ten years and have never had to use ice. It's a waste of money," the fishing captain sat back down.

A man in the audience called out, "The fish buyers should pay for the ice. They ship it."

Then Billy Adams stood up and said, "I think you men need to look at the bigger picture. We want to get better prices. Fish are trucked out of town now instead of by train and our product is going further. We'll get more money for our fish if we keep it iced. We give the association one cent and get five cents more per pound in return. Who doesn't want that?" He stopped to catch his breath. His muscular frame expanded as he took a deep breath and continued. "I say why not. Let's go for it." He sat down. There was some hand clapping and a couple whistles.

The gavel banged against the oak block. The president continued, "We can wait until next meeting to decide on taking a penny a pound. No vote will be taken tonight. Talk among yourselves and we'll vote at next meeting. Let's move on." After the business was concluded, the association president introduced "You all know Chief James Crowley," he said.

The chief walked to the front of the room. He liked these men, their sense of humor, and the gusto for life that seemed to exude from their mannerisms and speech. "I know you have better things to do than to listen to what I have to say, so I'll make this brief." A short hoot came from the back of the room.

"Billy Adams came to see me about my support for a dance. I want you all to know that I will speak to the Selectmen in favor of the association holding a fish fry and a dance at the end of the month. It is my understanding that you will be gifting part of the profits to charity and I find that commendable."

Crowley took a breath, looked around the room at the familiar faces, and continued, "The only thing that I ask is that if you are consuming alcohol, you will imbibe with care. We have had accidents involving vehicles. A horse cart was pushed off the road last summer. A few fights have been reported. These incidents can be blamed on too much to drink."

Laughter was heard around the room that suddenly subsided. "Maybe some of you remember when there wasn't one liquor store in Provincetown. We don't want a honky-tonk town."

Crowley knew that domestic violence was also a problem, one that was not addressed openly. He'd seen the results. If he could get the men to think about how much they consumed perhaps he could curtail some of the abuse that went along with it.

He continued, "I don't mean you shouldn't have a good time, hell, I hope to enjoy myself there as well. Let's keep it safe at the dance and safe on the roads going home. Thanks for letting me speak here this evening." There were a few cheers, some clapping, but mostly the men wanted to end the meeting and get home.

Crowley finished his speech and headed for the back of the room to retrieve his coat and hat. Billy Adams was standing near the door. "Hi Billy. I agree with what you had to say, the fishing boats using ice." The chief continued to talk as Billy moved toward the door. "This Association is good for the whole town." Crowley meant what he said. "The fishermen should be proud of all they've accomplished." Crowley waited for a reply.

Billy didn't look at Crowley. His head bobbed and he looked over the chief's shoulder at the men in the room. The fisherman wasn't interested in a conversation. "Yeah, I guess,"

"Well, I'd better be going. Nice to see you Billy." Crowley sensed that Billy was in a hurry. Fishermen surrounded the chief, shook his hand, and thanked him for coming, while the Chief watched Billy close the door.

By the time Crowley pulled his slicker over his shoulders and went out into the spring rain, Billy Adams was gone. The chief thought about how difficult it must be to get up at 3 o'clock in the morning, work on a moving boat all day, and then attend a meeting in the evening. Crowley had witnessed the problems that fishermen faced, away for long hours, sometimes no money for weeks, and some of the men drank heavily.

As the chief made his way out of the building and down the wet stairs he remembered Matt Rozon a few weeks back. A neighbor heard screaming and called the station. Mr. Rozon, skinny as a beanpole, pants hanging from suspenders, was waving a shotgun around, threatening to send his wife to kingdom come.

The moon cast light on a half empty bottle of whiskey lying on the ground next to a wooden barrel.

Mrs. Rozon, wearing a threadbare nightgown, was screaming obscenities at him. It was a volatile situation that could go very wrong at any moment. Matt was drunk. The chief spoke slowly, his tone firm. "Mrs. Rozon please, be quiet. Matt, I need you to put the gun down."

Rozon looked at him with unfocused eyes, swaying on his legs like he was on the deck of a rolling ship. Crowley walked right up to him and took the shotgun from his hands. The man didn't even seem to notice. Crowley asked the wife if she wanted her husband to spend the night in custody, but she said, "No, he'll be ok. He'll sleep it off." Crowley took the gun with him. The next morning a very humble fisherman appeared at the police station asking for the return of his shotgun. The two men had a long talk about the effects of alcohol. Matt agreed to lay off the booze and get help from the minister of the Methodist Church., which he did.

Alcohol played a part in some of the calls that his department received from the wharf. It was known that many fishermen drank to keep warm, to ease the pain from rheumatism, or to keep up their strength. When the boat hit the docks to unload, a captain or crewman would finish the day with a half-pint or more of whiskey. Crowley wondered how a man could drink that much and remain on his feet, much less keep fishing. Crowley had seen first hand how good men will sometimes turn nasty from too much alcohol.

The town's fishermen were a feisty, fiery group who Crowley had come to love and admire. The men in the room that night were welcoming and friendly, sharing stories and dilemmas, treating him with respect and courtesy.

Crowley crossed Commercial Street heading for the office to make a phone call. When he reached the cement steps that led to the basement office he glanced up and watched a pick up truck pass in front of the town hall. He saw Billy Adams hunched over the steering wheel, heading west, instead of in the direction of his home. Billy Adams was a hard working young man.

Crowley stepped into a puddle at the bottom of the steps as he unlocked the door to the Police Station. He looked at the clock, eight-thirty, still early enough to call. He picked up the receiver and asked the operator to put him through to the Alter residence. "One moment," she said. There was some clicking sounds, then ringing and then an answer.

"Hello, Alter residence." It was Susan.

"Hi," the chief said. "It's James Crowley. I was wondering if I could ask you to accompany me to dinner and a movie? Saturday if you're not busy." He had decided the direct approach would be best.

Her voice was soft with a happy note. In a teasing manner she answered, "Hi James, this is a surprise. I'm glad you called." There was no hesitation as she continued, "Yes, I'd like that. I hear there's a John Garfield movie playing, *Dust Be My Destiny*. Have you heard of it?" Crowley said no and asked what it was about. She continued, "It's with Priscilla Lane about a man and woman in love, struggling to live in a world that seems to be against them. I hear it's the cat's pajamas. I was hoping to see it."

Crowley groaned inwardly. He had hoped for a Hop-A-Long Cassidy western. "Swell, I'll pick you up at 5:30. We can have a bite to eat before going."

Chapter 11

After a night of little sleep, Crowley received news. "We have a positive identification from the landlady that your John Doe is Frank White," Shiff spoke into the phone like he'd had too little sleep as well. Shiff seldom identified himself on the telephone. He felt it was a waste of time. "I still have a man in Provincetown, but you're in charge down there, so I'll concede to your decision. What's it to be?"

Crowley knew exactly what the Boston policeman was asking. He said, "Since we know who John Doe is, I'd say your man should follow the guy who took the box. His name is Joseph Kurtz. He has lived with his wife at 29 Nickerson Street for three years."

The investigation now had direction. Crowley continued, "This will give Mr. Kurtz time to meet with others of like mind." Crowley wanted to talk to Kurtz, but it was too soon. The chief didn't think Kurtz would run, especially if he didn't know he was being followed.

"Knowing who our victim is and the connection to Kurtz, well, that could get us more information. Let's see where this leads," Crowley said. "I'll wait to impound the Oldsmobile until after Kurtz leaves on his next trip out of town. If anyone asks, I'll say it was abandoned." The chief wanted to give Shiff as much time as he could.

"Deal." The Boston detective then added, "I'll have my man keep an eye on the house. Kurtz drives a Chevy, four-door sedan. I ran Kurtz and White through our system this morning. There are no tickets, no infractions, no warrants, and no arrests. Both men are model citizens." There was sarcasm in his words.

Shiff didn't want this man to slip through his fingers either. "Both of them traveling salesmen, it's pretty much a forgone conclusion that they have something to do with the Brown Shirts. He doesn't look the type to randomly steal from a parked car, but you never know. How it ties into your victim is another matter. I'll keep you posted as to his whereabouts. We can pick him up after we see where those pamphlets are headed," Shiff stopped speaking.

Crowley didn't like that a possible murderer was leaving town. His thoughts were interrupted by Shiff who said, "And James, don't worry. We'll keep him under constant surveillance. We'll get him." Their agendas were different but they wanted the same thing. Justice. They didn't say goodbye, Shiff just hung up the phone.

Crowley pulled at the tip of his mustache, walked to the board, and removed the card that read John Doe. It now read FRANK WHITE. He read his notes for the hundredth time. He wrote: motive? Maybe the dead man was the boss. Or he was working for Kurtz, but what could have caused things to go wrong? Maybe it was about money, blackmail. Did Kurtz have means, opportunity, and motive? Crowley was determined to find all three. He needed to speak to Doc Rice again to see if he had any lead on the weapon.

The phone reminded him of dumbbells, and for some reason they felt heavy. He tapped the button on the cradle three times and the operator asked what number. "Tillie, Crowley here, get Doctor Rice for me, please." The doctor's wife was also his secretary, nurse, and all around helper, even though she had just turned seventy years old. She kept a careful record of every patient that came in, reason for the visit, and how they paid. Some never paid, but she kept track of that as well.

Crowley asked Mrs. Rice if the doctor was busy. "He's always busy." Came the reply. "He'll call when he's finished with this patient."

Ten minutes later the phone was ringing. "Chief Crowley," he said.

"What is it now?" the doctor sounded rushed. "I've got a waiting room full."

"I wanted to know if you've made any progress on the murder weapon?" Crowley asked.

"I've narrowed it down some. I'll come by your office around 4 o'clock. I should be done here by then, barring emergencies." The doctor hung up before Crowley could confirm, but it didn't matter, he'd be at the office when Dr. Rice arrived.

A few minutes later Chief Crowley and Lewis were seated across the desk from each other. "It's a match," Crowley said. "The victim is Frank White." Both men nodded their heads.

"That's great news," Lewis said. "Now all we have to do is figure out who killed him." Lewis had applied for the position at the police department along with others who had more experience. The chief liked that Lewis was from Provincetown. He knew the people, the lay of the land, and kept a close eye on the comings and goings around the wharfs. He was easy going, people trusted him, and he had already proved his resourcefulness. He was recommended by Crowley to the Board of Selectmen and got the job. That was five years ago.

"When I get the call that Kurtz has left town, I'd like you to call Duarte Motor's. Have Joe tow the Olds. I don't want it seen from the street. Tell Joe Duarte that I want it out of sight of the road. If he has any questions tell him to call me. I'm sure he's going to want to know who's going to pay for his services." Lewis went back to his desk.

Crowley spent the next hour making notes on a pad of paper about the victim. He was from Gloucester, drove an expensive car, and he was part of the Brown Shirt movement. He may have worked for Kurtz. Or maybe it was the opposite and White was Kurtz's boss? Crowley wondered if the FBI had a list of Nazi sympathizers? Would Crowley recognize any of the names? Why was Frank White in Provincetown? Why would Kurtz murder the man? Motive? "Too many unanswered questions," Crowley said out loud.

Doctor Rice entered the chief's office later that day, without knocking. "James, I've narrowed it down some. I made a drawing of the length, width, and the angle of penetration. I believe the weapon could be a chisel or woodworking tool of some sort." The doctor looked at Crowley to see if he had any questions. He continued, "A definite match will only come when you find the weapon, but as it stands now, I'm just guessing. Sorry but that's about as close as I can get." He handed the drawings and his notes to the chief.

Crowley thought the doctor looked tired, older, and there was weariness in his voice. "You've done a great job, doc. I appreciate all you do for us." The older gentleman gave a weak smile. Crowley continued, "We've been friends for a long time, doc, what's bothering you? Is it this murder?"

"Oh hell no. I don't like homicide any more than you, but it doesn't keep me awake at night. My son, Robert has gone and joined the Army. He'll be stationed in North Carolina, but if we get into conflict, who knows what can happen. Of course I'm against us getting into war, but everything seems to be pointing toward the fight. Certainly France and England are having a tough time of it. Aw, listen to me. I'm just tired, worried about Robert. I wish he'd waited. He could be going to Yale in the fall." Doc Rice finished and shook his head.

"Anything I can do doc, just ask," the chief said. Then added, "Like father, like son. He's a good man."

Rice said he had to go. The men shook hands and Crowley opened the office door for the elderly man. He returned to his desk.

Crowley pressed a button on the phone and Lewis picked up. The chief asked, "I was wondering if Joe Kurtz has a wood shed, a barn, or out building in his yard, a place where he'd keep tools?

Do you happen to know?" Lewis said he could call his cousin who lives near there and find out. The chief said no, not at this time. "I don't want any civilian help with this. I don't want information filtering into the town's gossip mill. On another note, how would you like a little over time?"

Lewis said he was interested and would do whatever was needed. Crowley continued, "When Joe Kurtz leaves his house the State Police will have a man following him. I want you to keep an eye on the house after he leaves. Have a discrete look around, see if there is a shed, but don't get caught sneaking around. Can you do that?"

Lewis replied that he'd be glad to do it. "I'll watch the place like a hawk and do a little night prowling when the time is right. Don't worry chief, I won't let you down."

Crowley smiled. "We can borrow a car for you to sit in. That will make it easier. I'd like you to stay sharp, but not be seen. The squad car is too well known."

"I'll borrow my cousin's old Ford for the night. Give him a dollar and tell him I've got a date. He won't ask questions."

Crowley agreed. "Wait until it's dark. Park close enough to see the house, but not so close that anyone would wonder what your doing there. If something comes up that you think may be important, phone me at home. No matter what time it is." Lewis said he would. The chief hesitated then added, "You're a good officer Lewis, thanks for all your help."

The younger man nodded. His ears turned bright red as he answered, "Just doing my job."

Chapter 12

Joe Kurtz left his house late Thursday afternoon. He got into his Chevrolet Standard Six that was parked at the side of his home and drove up Nickerson Street. Another vehicle, a 1933 Ford pulled out and followed as the Chevy turned onto Bradford Street. The two-lane road had traffic in both directions, but Harry concentrated on only one car.

After forty minutes, the lead car pulled into the town of Orleans and stopped in front of the *Whydah Tavern*. Joe Kurtz got out and went into the restaurant. The Boston officer drove past the tavern. He turned the car around and pulled into the parking area. He sat in his vehicle and waited. When nothing happened after fifteen minutes, he got out of the car and entered the tavern.

The room had a low ceiling. A long bar ran along the left wall. Tables on the right side of the room were occupied with June tourists enjoying supper. Harry went to the bar. He lifted one foot onto the brass rail that ran the length of the forty-foot polished wooden counter. Two stools away sat another customer sipping a beer, staring at the wall of bottles behind the bar. "What can I get you?" The barkeep asked.

Harry took off his hat and pushed his hair down with his right hand. "How much for a glass of beer." When told, he grumbled about how the price of everything was going through the roof. "Imagine paying twenty cents for a beer. It was only a dime last year. That's double."

The bartender shrugged, "It is what it is. Should I pour or not?" The new customer put two dimes on the bar. The barkeep poured the draft, and then walked to the other end of the bar, wiping the counter as he went.

"I know what you mean," the man on his right, two seats

down said. "Things are changing fast and I don't like it one bit." A hamburger was delivered to Kurtz who wiped his mouth between the large bites. During the meal he talked between bites about the taxes that were now being foisted on the public and the way the politicians were handling the money. "It's like they get to do whatever they want with our tax dollars. I'm fed up with how this country is being run."

Politics was a topic that could not be avoided. Harry stepped closer and introduced himself. "I'm Harry T. Enos." The undercover cop put out his hand. "I couldn't agree more," he said.

The other man shook his hand and said, "Joe Kurtz. I sell Fuller Brushes." He took another bite, chewed, and then added, "Can't even get a decent job. The Jews control the good jobs and they ain't giving work to the people who needs 'um."

"I know what you mean." Harry said. "I've been out of work for a month now and if things don't improve I don't know what I'm going to do." Harry was his first name but his last name was not Enos. If possible he would get on the good side of Joe Kurtz. Harry said that he'd been selling Hudson cars but the market had gone flat. "Ford, General Motors, and Chrysler have taken more than eighty percent of the automobile market. Now I'm out of work because of them." Harry said.

Joe Kurtz smiled. Harry continued, "Put us right out of business. Big corporations are taking over. The little guy doesn't stand a chance." Joe Kurtz ordered another beer and told the barman to give one to his neighbor.

Harry thanked him, leaned on the bar and sipped from his beer.

"I have a feeling that the US of A will be out manned, out gunned and out of luck if they decide to take up arms against Germany," Joe Kurtz said.

Harry felt his stomach turn, too much beer, and too much Joe Kurtz. He stuck to his role. "Yea, this country is going in the wrong direction real fast. We need to have a voice in government and make things happen to help the working people." He raised his glass as if in toast. His drinking partner nodded his head. Harry felt that their first meeting was going rather well.

"We should throw our weight in support of the fatherland," Kurtz said. Harry listened. Every once in a while nodding his head. After an hour of this kind of talk Joe Kurtz looked Harry over, from top to bottom as if sizing him for a coffin. "There's a meeting tonight. I think you may find it to your liking. I can introduce you to some people." Again there was a smile, big yellow teeth filling his face. "I'll bet it would be right up your alley. Are you interested in coming?"

"Sure, why not. I'm not doing anything else. Maybe I can find a job." Harry agreed. "I'll follow you." It was Harry's turn to smile.

It took less than ten minutes to drive to the meeting place. Harry parked next to a barn at the back of a private residence off Tonset Road going toward East Orleans. The barn, unseen from the road, was situated behind a white house with black shutters. Lights burned in the first floor windows. The dirt parking area contained two cars, a small panel van and a Ford pickup truck. Joe waited for Harry in front of the large gabled building. He held out his hand as a gesture of friendship and camaraderie. They shook hands. "I think your going to like what you hear tonight."

Joe led the way to a side entrance. The barn smelled of horse and hay. The place was cleared years ago of any animals that may have been in residence. The rafters were thirty feet from a packed-dirt floor that had been swept. Six rows of folding chairs faced a podium like the kind found in libraries that support dictionaries. Joe told Harry to take a seat.

Harry watched Kurtz carry a cardboard box to the front staging area. He placed it on a chair next to a man wearing a brown shirt and black tie. Harry watched them shake hands. Words were spoken that Harry couldn't hear and then the sharp eyes of the man in the brown shirt looked in Harry's direction. They nodded to each other.

Joe Kurtz came back to Harry and said, "I'd like to introduce you to someone."

They walked to the podium. Harry put out his hand, "I'm Harry T. Enos."

The other man squinted his eyes, looked Harry over carefully, taking his time. He said, "What brings you here tonight, other than Joe?"

Harry explained he was looking to better his life. "I'm out of work and fed up with the way things are heading in the country. I lived through the Great Depression. It was tough." Harry looked at the man in the brown shirt, their eyes met briefly before continued. "Then I got a job selling Hudson cars, but the dealership went belly-up, thanks to GM, Ford and Chrysler." Harry felt like he was under a magnifying glass. The other two men seemed to be taking in every inch of him and he was glad he'd left his 38 Special under the seat in the car.

"They don't give the little guy a chance. Anyway, I got to talk'n with Joe and found I agreed with what he was saying. We've got a lot in common. Damn Jews and Niggers getting better jobs than hard-working white folks. It's just not right." It was the right thing to say to this man in the black tie, but it actually pained Harry to say it.

The leader put out his hand for Harry to shake. Harry did. "We're glad to have you here tonight. Have a seat. People will be arriving shortly. Take one of these and read through it. I think you'll agree that it's time that America take steps in the right direction." The man was tall and thin with a pencil mustache above his lips. He never introduced himself and Harry had a feeling he would not learn his name tonight. It was going to be a long, unpleasant evening.

The barn filled with about a dozen people, all men. There

were a few handshakes, but no one spoke to Harry. The meeting began when the boss stood behind the podium and scanned the crowd. "I'm glad to see you all here tonight." The speech was what Harry expected. "Since passing the sixteenth amendment in 1913, that gave the government the right to tax our income, Congress keeps adding on more, so that a working man has to give over to the government much of his earnings. Taxes keep going up and this is unfair to the working people. Are we going to support a government that gives us nothing in return?" There was tepid applause from the audience.

He continued, his voice forceful, "Germany is strong." He pounded his fist on the wooden surface in front of him. "Poland is now a part of the Fatherland and it is growing as I speak. The government of the United States is weak. A third party is needed to wake Americans up from their apathy. That party should be the Third Reich. There are many people who are unhappy with the current politics. The time for getting our party members elected to higher office is now." The man wiped his brow with a white handkerchief, leaned forward, and smiled at the audience.

His words seemed to be absorbed into the dirt floor. He picked up speed and force as his toxic speech flew across the room. "We need to unite, get involved, and protest. We can take charge, bring America to its senses." The applause was sharper, with volume and encouragement. Harry's hands came together but without making much of a sound. The speech continued on the same note for fifteen minutes. At the end of the talk, the leader raised his right arm. "Hail Hitler," he said.

Everyone in the room responded with a similar gesture. Harry lifted his arm as if it were broken. People began standing, moving toward the door, shaking the hand of the man in the front with the black tie, and taking pamphlets from the box. The scene reminded Harry of high school graduation where the kids line up to receive their diploma from the head master. Harry looked at each man as they took the pamphlets and walked to the side entrance, trying to memorize the faces. He recognized no one.

Harry made his way to the front and took a few of the leaflets. "OK if I take a few?" he asked.

Joe was standing behind him. "Be careful who you give them to. And watch what you say. Not everyone is as forward and progressive in their thinking as those of us here tonight." Kurtz was looking around the room as he spoke. They walked back to their cars together using the lights from departing vehicles to find their way. Joe continued, "Our party is building a future for this country and there are many who think as we do, but we have enemies. Get my drift?"

Harry said he understood. He then asked Joe if he would see him again? "I have business further up the Cape tonight," Kurtz said. "There's another meeting next week." He hesitated, looked at the new party member, his eyes narrowing with suspicion. Harry wondered if he had asked the wrong question. Then Joe surprised Harry. "You own that car, right?"

Harry nodded. "It's the only thing I have left."

Kurtz's continued. "Would you be interested in some delivery work? I had a man, but he's," Kurtz stopped mid sentence and looked around the yard.

The wind rustled leaves in the trees. They could hear the sound of cars leaving the driveway, turning onto Tonset Road. Kurtz continued, "He's changed jobs. I'm looking for someone I can trust. How can I get in touch with you? "

"I can be trusted. If you don't mind my asking, how much will it pay?" Harry asked

"You'll earn enough." Kurtz asked Harry for a number where he could be reached. So Harry gave him a phone number in Provincetown.

Joe looked at him with renewed interest, squinting his eyes. "Isn't this a Provincetown exchange? I thought I knew everyone from that area. What are you doing here in Orleans?" His voice was sharp, too loud against the quiet night.

Harry was quick. "Yes, but it's temporary. I'm staying with my uncle. I went for a job interview in Hyannis today." A fleeting look of disappointment crossed his face. Harry looked at the ground as if embarrassed. "I didn't get the job and I don't have a place of my own. My only living relative and he's out on the end of a sand spit." Harry was making it up as he went along. "My wife left me a year ago. She went to live with her sister in New York." Joe Kurtz seemed to accept the story.

"Well then," a slow smile formed on Joe's thick lips, "this job might be right up your alley. I'll give you a call when I've got something lined up."

Harry got into his car and headed for Provincetown. He needed to see Chief Crowley right away. He would call Shiff from the chief's house and bring him up to date. He stepped on the gas pedal, feeling like he needed a hot bath.

Chapter 13

On Wednesday night while Joe Kurtz and Harry were at the barn in Orleans, Lewis sat in a Model T Ford watching the house at the end of Nickerson Street. Lewis borrowed the car from his cousin Jimmy Silva.

Ford stopped making the *Farmer's Car* as it was known, in 1927, but many remained running. Silva didn't mind lending it, especially since Lewis gave him a dollar to use it.

Lewis had the window rolled down to let in the mild breeze. He felt his head falling on his chest as he fought to stay awake. He figured he'd wait until after midnight to go exploring. There was no traffic. Three cars were parked on the left side of the street allowing enough room for other vehicles to pass. His car was the one in the middle.

A vehicle drove slowly up the street just before ten o'clock. Lewis heard the engine and saw the headlamps in his rear view mirror. He ducked down so that his eyes were level with the bottom of the windshield.

There were no streetlights this far out of town, but Lewis felt sure something was about to happen. He kept his eyes glued on number 29. The pickup truck stopped in front of the house. A man in boots and a fishermen's hat went to the door. The movement was quick and with the poor light Lewis didn't recognize the visitor, but the truck looked familiar.

Lewis was now wide-awake. "Crowley is going to love this." Lewis whispered. He sat in the car and waited, never taking his eyes off the house. An hour later the front door opened. The same man said a few words to Millie Kurtz. Their bodies came together in a seductive way. They kissed and then the man quickly left. It was too dark to see the man's face.

Lewis lay on the front seat unobserved when the truck rattled passed. It was the type of vehicle used by fishermen and farmers throughout town to haul produce and fish. The stranger turned left at the corner, onto Bradford Street. Lewis started the engine and headed in the same direction. He followed the truck to the center of town.

Once under the street lamps at the back of Town Hall, Lewis was sure he knew the driver. He followed and watched him go into a house on Standish Street. "Holy Smoke." Lewis said.

The patrolman parked at the rear of the Town Hall. Within a few minutes he had unlocked the police department door. He picked up the phone and asked the operator for 2121. The operator knew the number and plugged the call into the circuit board. "Crowley here," came the response after two rings.

"Chief, it's Lewis. I'm at the station. I have news. Do you want to hear it over the phone or should I come to your place." They both knew that to keep anything private they would have to avoid the local switchboard. Phone calls could easily be overheard.

"Come over. I'll make coffee." The chief hung up and ten minutes later he was sitting across from Lewis who was too excited to drink anything. His coffee cup sat on the kitchen table untouched.

Lewis told his boss everything. "I'm positive it was Billy Adams," he said. "I know him. He was in my class in grade school but left when he was sixteen to fish with his father."

The chief sipped his coffee and said nothing for a few minutes. He took a deep breath and let out an audible sigh. "Having an affair is not against the law, but I'm going to have a talk with him. My guess is he's up early. I'll see if I can catch him before he heads to his boat in the morning. This investigation is about more than romance."

The kitchen was quiet. "Let's see what Billy knows. If he spends time with Mrs. Kurtz maybe he will know something. We have to look at this case as many faceted, like an unpolished diamond. The more we polish the more information we get. And I intend to get to the heart of it."

Lewis scratched his head. "I hope Billy doesn't have anything to do with this Nazi stuff."

The chief smiled at the innocence that still clung to Lewis. "I doubt it. It looks more like his relationship with Mrs. Kurtz happens when Mr. Kurtz is gone to meetings."

They let that hang in the air, then Crowley continued, "Call Duarte Motors in the morning and have the Olds towed." He thanked Lewis for his hard work and sent him home to get a good night's sleep.

The chief thought about affairs of the heart. It wouldn't be easy to be involved in a relationship of this kind. They would have to stay out of prying eyes. The anxiety would be wearing. Crowley couldn't imagine such a relationship. A fleeting memory of Eleanor passed through his mind and that reminded him of his date with Susan. He was looking forward to seeing her again, up close, and personal, no secret rendezvous for them. She was a breath of fresh air.

His reverie was interrupted by a knock at the kitchen door. He drew aside the curtain on the window. The chief was surprised to see the same plainclothes officer that Detective Shiff had introduced to him. Crowley offered the man a cup of coffee. The Boston officer shook his head, no.

"I had to speak to you before I head back to the rooming house. I've been following Joe Kurtz. It's a long story and you don't need to know all the details." The chief knew what the man's job was, so he was not surprised by what the officer had to say. "I made contact with Kurtz this evening in Orleans and that led to me going to a Party meeting."

What Harry said next was the surprise. "I had to give the man a local phone number, one he can use to call me about a job.

I couldn't think of any number except yours, 2121. I'm sorry but I gave the man your home phone number." The two policemen looked at each other. There was a slight bobbing of the chief's head. He grunted and bit the tip of his mustache.

The Boston cop continued, "I know I should have been better prepared and I'm sorry about that. But I wasn't, and now I'm stuck, or rather we're stuck." Harry explained that Joe thought he was staying with his uncle in Provincetown. "Yours was the only number that I know."

Crowley took a moment to think about the situation. He didn't like it but realized that with a few adjustments they could use this to their advantage. They needed to work together. Crowley believed that Joe Kurtz held the key to the murder.

"OK, we can handle this. I'll answer the phone without using my name. Maybe even disguise my voice." Crowley chuckled at the idea.

Harry smiled and thanked him for his support. He turned toward the kitchen door, preparing to disappear into the night.

Crowley stopped him by saying, "Look, I have a spare room, why don't you get your overnight bag and stay here. That way you can answer the phone when he calls."

"Sounds great. I'll move my car to your back yard and grab my kit." He looked around the kitchen then added, "but do you have a bathtub. That meeting left my skin crawling, if you know what I mean." Crowley told him to make himself at home.

The Boston policeman used the phone to call his boss. He gave Shiff a run down on what had transpired. Everything was said in a type of code. "I went to a party this evening. Met some important people, got a job offer, so I won't go back to my old job. I'd like to keep in touch through our mutual friend." Shiff said he understood. Progress was being made.

Chapter 14

Spring at the end of the peninsula brought long shadows, green ground, and leaves to the Elm trees that shaded the streets throughout the town. The sun was still high in the sky in the late afternoon as Mildred sat with her husband Joe at their kitchen table. Neither noticed the blue sky or the warmth in the air.

She had made a chicken stew with dumplings. He ate with gusto, filling his mouth, slurping the food from a spoon. "You want more?" she asked. He was wiping up the gravy with a thick slice of homemade bread. He grunted and she thought he meant yes. She scooped another spoonful onto the plate.

"How was your sales trip?" Mildred asked about his work. He rarely talked about his daily routine or his business, but she always asked. She didn't know what else to talk about to this man who was more a stranger than a husband. He made noise, a grunting sound, but no words.

Mildred was moving food around on her dish. Again Joe grunted. It was a sound that his wife interpreted as not being important enough to require comment. He didn't wish to talk further on the subject. She picked up the dishes, put them in the sink, and then moved to the stove. After filling two cups with coffee she sat down across from the man she had married. Her expression was blank. It was difficult to tell what she was thinking and Joe never asked.

Joe was on the road more than he was home. She spent her days alone. Much to her surprise, she enjoyed the quiet. When her husband was home she withdrew. She had had a birthday the past week that went unnoticed. She was now twenty-seven years old. They had no children. She knew it was a loveless marriage.

Out of the blue Joe asked. "Have you heard anything about

that car that was parked up at the top of Nickerson Street? It was there two nights ago, but now it's gone. Do you know where it went?"

Mildred didn't understand the question. "What car? No, I don't know anything about a car. How would I know about a car parked on the street? I never leave the yard."

"Don't get snappy with me. I'm just asking a question, is all." Joe picked up the Advocate newspaper and went to the living room. It was always the same when he was home. He would read the paper and then call to her to join him in the bedroom to fulfill her wifely duties.

Mildred put her hands into the soapy dishpan in the sink, sighing, she looked out the window. A Crow was cawing from the top of a tree. "I wish I could fly." She whispered. She washed the dishes and went to the back door and sat on the steps that led to her small garden. Sprouts were appearing from the plants that she had seeded. The kale was already a foot high. She lit a cigarette, enjoying the smoke as it settled her nerves. Again she sighed. She was careful with the small amount of money her husband gave her and purchased only one pack every two weeks, making them last. When the tobacco was smoked to her fingertips she crushed the tip, buried it at the edge of the garden, and then went back into the house.

Millie was surprised when Joe spoke to her. She jumped. He told her that he was making progress at work. He'd made a little extra money that week and was saving it because he needed new tires for the truck. He gave her ten dollars, a week's worth of expenses for the house and then said, "It's time for bed." She knew what that meant. She turned off the light in the living room and followed her husband into the bedroom.

Mildred sat on the edge of the bed unbuttoning her dress. It was dark blue with white buttons that ran the entire length of the front. She liked this dress. Joe came out of the bathroom. He had taken off his shoes and was pulling the suspenders off his shoulders when a heavy knock sounded on the front door. "Now who the hell can that be," Joe said. Mildred began to close the top of her dress. She got to her feet to go to the door. Joe said, "You stay here."

She watched him leave the bedroom. Her husband turned on a light in the living room and opened the door. Mildred could hear loud voices coming from the front of the house. Joe sounded displeased but also scared. "What are you doing here? I thought we had an agreement. We weren't going to have contact at our homes."

Eddie the Enforcer was the nickname given to the man who waited to be asked in. Members of their group were uncomfortable around him, but he was the one they called when a strong arm was needed.

The man spoke with an accent. He was loud enough so that Mildred could hear some of the words. The stranger seemed annoyed. His voice was rough and she had to strain to understand what was being said. "Nevah mind dat. I've been sent by our friend to find out vhere is Frank." The Enforcer leaned his head toward the house as if to see inside. Mildred listened from behind the bedroom door.

Joe stood rigid, his body stiffened. Then his shoulders bent slightly as if he had caved in at the belly. His breathing was audible. "You'd better come in. My wife is in the bedroom so keep your voice down." The stranger entered. He towered over the homeowner and did not ask permission to sit, choosing Joe's armchair.

Joe pulled a straight back chair from under a desk and moved it closer to the intruder. "What's this all about? Make it fast and then get out." Joe straightened his back, knowing he had some authority, trying to appear as if he were in charge. It didn't seem to faze his unwanted guest.

He took a cigarette from behind his ear. There was silence as the stranger lit a cigarette. The sound of a match scratching against sandpaper was followed by a gust of wind that blew out the flame. "The boss vants answers. He said to me, 'Go see Joe.' He thinks you know vhere he's gone. He vants Frank. What's he up to?" Ed put a meaty hand into the inside pocket of his jacket causing Joe to lean away from the man.

Eddie saw the fear in his eyes and chuckled. He pulled out a pack of Pall Mall, offering one to Joe who shook his head. "Vhen someone with all his knowledge about our organization doesn't show up for vork the boss wants to know vhy."

The man spoke with a sweet sound. He leaned closer to Joe and blew smoke in his face. "Boss thinks you vere the last person to see him. Get my drift, Joey?" The words seemed slurred, using a v instead of w. The word *get* sounded like git as in gitty-up. The sneer on his lips was easy to read.

Joe looked toward the bedroom door before he spoke, his words a whisper. "I don't know what you're talking about. I haven't seen him. Not since the meeting in Orleans, over a week ago, at Smitty's house. I thought you drove off with him that night. Maybe the boss should be asking you the same questions."

Ed was quick to reply. His voice grew louder. Joe could smell cigarettes and booze on his breath. "Vhere you get that box you brought to the barn? Boss need to know." Joe hesitated and looked around the room.

Mildred pulled away from the door when her husband looked toward the bedroom. She couldn't resist staring at the large man through the crack the door. He was sitting with his back to her. He was bigger than her husband. He wore a Fedora hat pulled down to his eyebrows and hadn't bothered to remove it. She couldn't see his face, but he was husky, wide shoulders, and arms bulging inside his grey pinstriped suit. He appeared powerful. She stood motionless, only her eyebrows moved as they creased with suspicion and fear.

"I haven't seen him," Kurtz said. "I noticed the car parked on the street, it looked like Frank's, so I had a look inside. The box was on the front seat. I recognized it, so I took it." His eyes were moving from the Enforcer to the front door as if he thought maybe he could escape before the big guy got to him, an impossible feat.

Joe tried to placate Eddie. He continued, "Listen, I thought Frank might be shacking up with some floozy. I figured that he'd picked up a chickie and was staying around here. You know how it is. We needed the pamphlets, so I took the box from the Olds. No harm in that." There were beads of sweat on Joe's upper lip and the armpits of his undershirt were damp. "But I didn't see him, honest." he said.

Eddie sat motionless. A clock ticked. He puffed on the cigarette for a few minutes then dropped it in a cup that sat on the table. The butt hissed as it died out. The house seemed strangely quiet, eerie. Mildred shivered.

The men stood up. She could hear their footsteps as they moved toward the front door. Eddie the Enforcer had one last remark. "Next meeting the boss vant answers. Find out where is his car? Get it?"

Joe was trying to remember if there was anything he could tell the man to keep him moving toward the door. He said, "When I got back today around four o'clock the Oldsmobile was gone. I assume he came and got it. You're going to have to look for him in Gloucester. That's where he lives."

The other man made a throaty grunting sound. Mildred thought it sounded like the gorilla she had seen at the circus in Hyannis last summer. He put his hand on the doorknob. "The boss, he's not going to like this."

As the door closed, Mildred let out the breath she was holding. She didn't know exactly what had happened or who the man was, but she knew she didn't like what she had seen. Aware that there were things her husband hadn't told her, things that she didn't understand, or want to know about, she felt fear tug at her heart. They both kept secrets. Now she knew some of his, but he didn't know any of hers.

When Joe returned to the bedroom. Mildred was in the bathroom with the water running. The bed squeaked as he sat. The water stopped running. Joe was pulling on his shoes. "Mildred, I'm going out," he hollered.

Standing at the bathroom door Mildred asked, "At this hour? Who was that man?" Joe looked at her but didn't answer. Then she asked, "Where are you going? Will you be back tonight?"

"I'm going downtown to have a drink at the Governor Bradford. Don't wait up." He put his shirt on over his damp armpits, pulled up his suspenders, took a jacket from the rack next to the door and left without another word. She watched out the front window. Joe got into his car, turn it around and head back out Nickerson toward Bradford Street. There was no light in the front window that night.

Chapter 15

Mildred was glad to see him leave. She now knew that her husband was involved with people who frightened Joe, and that was something she would not have guessed. She sat in the dark kitchen and lit a cigarette. She hated being married, hated the secrets she carried, hated her life.

She thought about Billy Adams. He was the only good thing that had ever happened to her. Billy, with his bright smile, dark hair and boyish manner had appeared in her back yard one afternoon in early March. She remembered that day three months ago as if it were yesterday. It was a sunny, windy day and she had on the same blue dress.

She was alone, hanging laundry on the line in the back yard when Billy showed up. He had a fish on a string in his hand and he startled her. He had been watching her. He told her he was looking for Mrs. Costa to bring a fish to her. The fisherman grinned as he looked at her. "I was told she lives on Nickerson and can't make it into town due to her age." He raised the Codfish that he intended to give to the old woman.

Mildred blushed. "You've gone right by Mrs. Costa's house. She lives closer to Bradford Street, on the left side as you go back. I think it's number nineteen. This is twenty-nine. It's the house with yellow shutters." He smiled and shrugged his shoulders.

Mildred's home backed up against scrub pine. Wild roses were in bloom. Sand dunes surrounded the weathered building on three sides. It seemed an isolated spot, even with neighboring houses further up the street.

"I'm sorry. Didn't mean to bother you." Billy said. He introduced himself. "I'm Billy Adams. When no one answered my knock at the front door I just naturally came around back. I was thinking of old Mrs. Costa and I didn't expect to see such a pretty sight."

Mildred hadn't talked to another adult in two days. She blushed. "I know who you are. I'm Millie Sewall, now Mrs. Kurtz, but I don't expect you'd remember me. You were ahead of me in school." She had removed two clothespins from her pocket, hung up a shirt and then looked at the basket at her feet. "Can I get you a drink of water?"

He said no, that he didn't want to bother her. She said it wasn't a bother and he accepted a glass of water. They had noticed each other in passing over the years, but they didn't know one another. They were strangers that happened to live in the same small town.

He didn't leave the fish. "Oh, it's much too big for me," she said, blushing for no apparent reason. He didn't stay long, about ten minutes, but there was a desire, raised blood pressure, and a tingle of excitement felt by both. Their affair began with passion and was unexpected as these things surely are.

Mildred married Joseph Kurtz when she was twenty-four years old. She was pretty, but self-conscious. She had grown up poor, never had enough to eat, always cold, and was rarely given any affection. Her parents died during a flu epidemic of 1918. Mildred was left alone at the age of eighteen. She worked as a cleaning woman at the Pilgrim House and was given a small room by the owners who took the rent out of her pay. She was a hard worker and was given the opportunity to wait tables in the dining room during the summer months. It was a step up for her, the tips a bonus. That's where she met Joe Kurtz. He took her out to eat, spent money on gifts for her, and told her repeatedly how pretty she was.

She was a romantic, naive woman who had dreams of being swept off her feet, of being given fervent, passionate love. Their marriage turned out to lack substance. There was no passion. It wasn't long before he stopped taking her out and stopped buying gifts. She was bewildered by his roughness and the displeasure she saw in her husband's eyes. Both were dissatisfied with their lives. There was no laughter, no dreams fulfilled, and no love at the house on Nickerson Street. Mildred quickly became used to being alone. She didn't mind that her husband was secretive about what he did and where he went. She didn't ask questions.

There was enough money to support them so Joe made her quit her job as a waitress. She planted a garden, went for walks across the dunes, and sometimes stopped at St. Peter's Church to say a prayer. Her life wasn't bad, just empty.

When Captain Billy Adams, a strong healthy fisherman with strong healthy appetites, showed up in her back yard something exploded inside her. "I'd better get this fish to Mrs. Costa," he had said. In the back yard, sitting on an overturned barrel, she watched his body as he walked away, wide shoulders, strong arms, and a swagger in his hips. He turned and smiled at her before leaving the yard. Her breath caught in her throat.

A few days later he was back. She was in the kitchen at the table making a list of supplies that she needed delivered from the market. There was a knock on the back door and there he stood on the steps with a smile on his lips and a fish on a string in his hand. "I brought this for you, it's a bit smaller," he said.

Millie stepped back, beaming, and let him into the kitchen. "Thank you," she said. Put it in the sink." The room was crowded. To get to the sink he had to brush past her. Their bodies touched. It was sudden. The fish landed in the sink. Billy and Millie landed in each other's arms. Their desire created an intense heat. Waves of passion rolled over them. The space between them was filled with hot breath, moans, and an ache so deep that it needed to be put to rest before it crushed them.

His mouth covered hers. She tasted so sweet he thought he'd died and gone to heaven. There was nothing slow about their coming together and it was just the beginning. The experience left her feeling as if she were floating on the wings of angels. Tears sprang to her eyes, but she laughed. They kissed again and again.

They were seated at the table a short time later. He had a shy grin on his face. She explained that her husband wasn't expected back until late that evening or maybe not until the next day. They sat at the kitchen table and talked until Billy said, "I'd better go." She didn't try to stop him. "Can I come back?" he asked. The fisherman was aggressive, worked hard for what he had, but spoke in a soft melodic voice as if singing the words, pleasing and tender. Millie wanted more.

The house seemed extraordinarily quiet for a few minutes while the question hung in the air. The window was open and they could hear birds singing, tweeting and chirping their calls. He took her hand in his and held it.

She spoke, whispering, "I'll light a small lamp in the front window when it is safe, day or night. Be sure that his car is gone. If there is no light please stay away. If the lamp is lit, it will mean that my husband is not home and that I don't expect him."

And so the affair began. After three months she knew she loved him and would do anything for him.

The last time they were together was on a magical June evening, one that she would always remember. The smell of wild roses filled the spring air. The sun had not yet set. Red, orange and violet splashed across the sky. They had a blanket and walked over the dune in the back of the house. Billy spread the clothe across the sand. They lay inside a hollow, an indentation in the dune shaped like a teacup. They talked, laughed, and made love. It was so special. She felt her heart squeeze when she thought about it.

Now she worried that the time they had together was coming to an end and it was becoming more and more difficult to let go.

Chapter 16

Billy found his way to the end of Nickerson Street each night before heading home. Whenever the light was in the window and no sign of the car, he went around the back and tapped softly on the door.

On this night as every other night for the past three months, Billy drove his Ford down Nickerson Street. As always, he pulled over before reaching the house and looked for a light. What he observed was a 1935 Chevrolet Standard Six with Joe Kurtz behind the wheel driving toward him. Billy slid below the windshield as the car passed. The husband had a grim expression on his face, eyes squinting, jaw firmly set and with his hat pulled down across his forehead, he seemed oblivious of his surroundings.

Kurtz didn't look at the cars parked on the street, intent on some distant vision. Billy watched in the rear view mirror as Kurtz turned onto Bradford Street and was gone. Billy drove to the end of Nickerson Street and turned around. No light shown from the window.

That same Thursday evening Chief Crowley was sitting in his car on Standish Street across from the apartment that Billy Adams rented from Manny Brown. The chief had checked the waterfront. Billy's boat was tied alongside Fishermen's Wharf, but no one was onboard. His truck was not around. So like any good cop, Crowley waited, watching the house from the patrol car with the window rolled down while puffing on his favorite pipe. The sweet smell drifted around inside the '37 Chevy sedan clinging to the soft grey fabric surrounding his seat.

Twilight had passed taking the edges of light with it. It wasn't long before a truck pulled into a spot next to the white picket fence in front of the house. Billy got out. At the same time Crowley opened the squad car's door. The chief called Billy's name from across the street. The fisherman stopped and waited.

"I wonder if I could have a word with you?" The chief asked. "It'll only take a minute. Inside would be best." The chief nodded toward the front door.

"What's this about?" Billy asked, not moving from the side of his truck. "I've been fishing all day and I'm tired. Could this wait till tomorrow?" The fisherman had boots on his feet, a peaked fishermen's cap on his head, and a black rubber jacket flung over his shoulder.

"Sorry Billy. It's either in your apartment or it's at the station, but it's now." The chief's gaze searched the young man's face for resignation, compliance, or consent. None was forthcoming.

Billy bent his head, cast his eyes down, and took a breath. "OK, Come on up, if you want." A narrow stairway led to a converted attic apartment. At the top of the stairs Billy opened the door and flicked on the light.

Crowley stepped into the kitchen. The area contained a gas stove, sink and a small refrigerator. A table was pushed against the wall. There were two chairs. Everything looked neat, no dishes left out, no food or garbage to be seen. Billy dropped a bucket into the sink and then hung his jacket on the hook in back of the door. He slid his feet out of the boots and walked into the living room without saying anything. Crowley followed.

The fisherman turned on the lamp. He sat down, letting his body sink as if it were a heavy stone.

He let out a long, heavy breath. "OK Chief. What can I do for you?" Billy tried to sound aloof as if he were tired and didn't care what the reason was. It came out too loud. He didn't offer a seat, but Crowley sat on the small sofa anyway.

"I'd like to ask you about the Kurtz's." Crowley watched for a reaction. Billy twitched. He tried to look puzzled, but he looked more fearful, sharp eyes suddenly anxious. The chief looked straight at the fisherman.

"Kurtz?" Billy stopped. Then added, "I don't know the name." He was looking over the chief's shoulder at the wall.

Crowley didn't take his eyes off the fisherman. "Well, let me put it this way. I'm interested in Joe Kurtz. You're interested in his wife." The policeman waited and watched. He continued, "I figure you must know something about Mr. Kurtz." The chief waited. Now would be the right time for Billy to admit what was going on between him and Mrs. Kurtz. The chief tapped his fingers on his the side of the sofa.

"I don't know what you're talking about." Billy said. He was shaking his head from side to side and looking at the floor. His head came up quickly when he heard what the chief said next.

"I know about you seeing Mildred Kurtz when her husband isn't around. And frankly I don't care what two consenting adults are up to." The chief looked at the fisherman. "I'm here because I was hoping that maybe Mildred Kurtz may have said something to you, or maybe you saw something last Monday or Tuesday, something that might interest me. Understand? I'm looking for information about Joe Kurtz. Was he home on those days? What he's been up to, the places he goes, the people he meets."

The room was still. There was a tremor in his hand as Billy pulled a pack of cigarettes from his shirt pocket. He offered one to Crowley. Crowley shook his head and touched the pipe in the breast pocket. Billy got up and raised the window, letting in the southwest breeze. The salt air felt refreshing. Crowley waited for Billy to answer his question.

"I really don't know anything about Mr. Kurtz," Billy said after taking a large drag and letting the smoke curl out the side of his half opened mouth. "We don't discuss her husband."

"Do you know if he was at home on either of those nights?"

The fisherman was quiet. Crowley watched as Billy searched for an answer. "I'm not sure. Let me think for a minute."

The chief prodded, "That would be just a few days ago. There was no moon that night. Did you visit your friend on Monday or Tuesday evening? Was Joe at home on those nights?"

Billy didn't want to talk about his visits. "Can we leave Millie out of this?" He looked at the police chief, shifted in the chair, and took a drag on the Lucky Strike. "What's this all about, anyway?"

"Well Billy, it seems that Mrs. Kurtz's husband has been working with some very shady and dangerous people. I have reason to suspect that he is involved in some nasty business. He's a member of an organization that is not well liked, and I think he might know something about a man we are interested in, a man named Frank White."

Crowley stopped and looked at Billy, but the fisherman was looking out the window. The chief asked, "Has that name ever come up in your conversations?"

Billy's eyebrows came together. He put his cigarette out in the ashtray on the side table and looked at Crowley. "Never met Joe Kurtz and never heard of this Frank fellow? I didn't see Millie on either of those nights. And I don't know if her husband was home or not. I fished and was tired, came home from the boat and went to bed."

"Did Millie ever talk about her husband? Who his friends are? Where he went on his business trips, any plans he was making, things like that?" The chief waited, hoping for any information that could shed light on Joe Kurtz and his operation. "Did she ever mention Frank White?"

"I told you, we didn't talk about her husband or this other guy."

The police chief knew when to back off. He stood up. Billy continued speaking, "Chief? I hope you can keep this between us. I mean you're not going to say anything to Millie's husband, are you?" The fisherman had real concern written on his face. "He'd kill her if he ever found out. Please. Can you leave her out of this?"

Crowley wanted to reassure him, but couldn't. "I can't promise anything, but I certainly won't say anything unless I have no choice. Right now your relationship is not the focus of my investigation." Crowley softened his voice and looked straight at the fisherman. "I'm most likely going to have to talk to Mrs. Kurtz in the future, but not just yet. And if I were you, I'd stay away from her for the time being."

The chief walked toward the kitchen, stopped and turned. "If you think of anything that might help, give me a call at the station." He said good night and left the fisherman sitting in the chair lighting another cigarette.

Chapter 17

On his way home Crowley stopped at the station. Lewis had left one message for him. The coroner's report had arrived. There was nothing new in it. The wound in Frank White's back was eight inches deep, one inch in width. A knife was ruled out as being too thin. It may have been a tool of some sort, but the report did not identify the murder weapon. Crowley wrote the word WEAPON on a card, added a few words about the size of the wound, and stuck it under the one that said, Frank White. He would pester Dr. Rice in the morning.

Right now he needed to eat and get some sleep. Then he remembered his houseguest. The chief sighed, shook his head, and said out loud, "What I do in the name of the law."

Crowley parked the patrol car in a small clearing near the back door next to a vehicle already there. The house, a shingled and weathered Cape style with two dormers protruding from the roof, was built in 1800 and had been bequeathed to him by his mother's sister. James Crowley was her only surviving family member. The lights were on, giving Crowley a strange feeling. He didn't know if he felt welcomed or intruded upon, but once he opened the door, he was glad that he'd invited Harry to stay."

"Hey," the chief said. "Sure smells good in here." Crowley walked into his kitchen and found his new roommate wearing an apron over his faded undershirt. It was the one his aunt used to wear. It covered him from neck to knees, was tied at the back of his neck and around the waist.

Crowley had a smile on his face. He continued, "I didn't know I was getting a cook when I said I'd loan you my phone." He had to chuckle because the man had a wooden spoon in his hand and the room smelled like home cooking.

"Hi Chief. It's just a Bolognese sauce, my mom is a great cook, taught me all I know, and this is it," Harry said. "I hope you don't mind. I found everything I needed right here and I had time to kill while waiting."

"Not if it tastes as good as it smells." The chief put his hat on the side table, hung his jacket on a hook, and then pulled all the shades on the kitchen windows. "Did you get any phone calls while you were cooking?" Crowley poured himself a glass of water and sat at the table.

"As a matter of fact I am meeting Joe Kurtz at the Governor Bradford tonight at 9:30. He's got a job for me. I think I'll be heading out of town, so the house will be all yours again. Where do you keep the plates?"

Over bowls of pasta the two men discussed the sharp rise in crime, dissidents, and protest marches. Politics seemed to be pulling the country apart. There were those in favor of entering the war and those opposed. "We need more good men in law enforcement and we should have more time off," Crowley said. They both laughed at that.

"We had a rash of break-ins last winter," The chief added. There were complaints from residents who came to town for the summer months. He continued, "I've been told that the local kids are targeting the homes of the part time residence. Even if I caught the hooligans red handed, the only thing I could do is get their parents to pay to clean up the messes they make. They don't steal anything, just break in and make themselves at home. It's hard to catch them. They don't put on lights or build fires, but they eat whatever food is available and drink any booze they find. Catching them is low on my priority list."

The police chief was riding through town, up and down various streets at various hours of the day and night. "Checking the heartbeat of the town." He said, "Might help to curb some of their shenanigans if they know I'm looking. I had one part-time resident tell me it was my fault that his place was broken into. Imagine that. I told him to hire a security guard or get someone to live in his house for the winter. I know plenty of people who'd take the owner up on it." Crowley was shaking his head. "I can't be in all places at all times, besides and I've got a few other things on my plate right now.

Harry interrupted. "Well if it's any consolation the city is worse. Robbery and murder are up. We've had protest parades, violent marches, and our mayor, Maurice J. Tobin, is on the warpath. We don't have enough coverage and Shiff has got me working down here. Let's hope this little sting operation proves to be worth his efforts. If it doesn't pan out they'll be hell to pay."

They lingered over the empty dishes while smoking, the chief his pipe and Harry his cigarette. "You ever been married?" The Boston policeman asked.

"No never." Crowley answered, "Came close one time."

"What happened? Good looking guy like you should be happily married with seven kids by now."

The chief thought about his personal life. He didn't usually talk about his past, but for some reason, maybe the good meal or the company, he felt less inhibited. "My parents, along with millions of others, died from the Spanish Flu while I was at college. I lost both within days of each other. I was confused, angry, and didn't know which way to turn. I wanted to run. So I joined the Army. While I was overseas, the girl of my dreams married my best friend." James Crowley sat quietly.

He pictured Eleanor, her curly red hair, bright green eyes, her smile, and the way she moved through a room. He continued to be fond of her, her husband Manny, and their family. He continued, speaking truthfully, "It was for the best. I was gone for years. The Army made me cynical and not someone ready to marry. Eleanor and Manny have produced three beautiful daughters that I adore. And I still have my best friends."

He seldom felt jealous. He considered himself welcome in their home. "I was shipped to Europe in 1919 just as the war was ending. The Great War." He said the last three words with a sadness that seemed to roll from within him. He paused, remembering, before continuing. "I helped to clean up and to try to identify the dead. The destruction was unimaginable."

The kitchen was quiet. Outside an owl hooted, the open window let in the night air. "When I was discharged I didn't know what to do with myself. It really was a fluke that I went to the Police Academy, but that's a story for another time. When my parents died I lived with my aunt Philomena, in this very house. She left it to me when she passed. Eventually, I came back to my roots here in Provincetown. Just like they say in that new movie, *The Wizard of Oz*, there's no place like home."

No one spoke for a few minutes, each with thoughts of love, lost and found. The silence was broken by Crowley. "How about you? Got a wife, or girl?" The chief let his thoughts fall into the abyss as he concentrated on his dinner partner.

"There is a young lady in Boston. She lives in the North End. Angela is her name. We've dated for about a year now. I think it's serious. I might even pop the question when this operation with our Nazi friends is over." The Boston cop smiled shyly. "Who knows, she may say yes." They laughed.

Crowley picked up the plates and rinsed them at the sink. "Thanks, I needed that. Any time you want to stay here, just say the word." The chief patted his stomach and then said, "I think for the time being I'll continue to answer the phone without introducing myself. And I'll have a word with our local switchboard operator. I think for the time being, it would be safer." The two men discussed the possibility of someone checking up on Harry.

The Chief put the leftovers in the icebox and said, "I do a pretty good imitation of an old man. No one will recognize my voice when I answer the phone." The two men were enjoying the respite from more serious matters. They shook hands. And said goodbye. "If I don't see you in the morning, stay safe, warm and dry," Crowley said. Harry went to meet Joe Kurtz.

Chapter 18

The Governor Bradford Restaurant and Bar, located in the center of town, is a place where locals go to eat, listen to the radio, and sometimes dance to the Portuguese Band. A shellacked bar, reflecting the lights that hung above it, took up the left side of the room. Harry scanned the place taking note of the red barstools, spittoons on the floor and a bartender polishing glasses. Dinner was over, the tourists gone, and a waitress was wiping down empty tables.

Joe Kurtz sat alone at the end of the bar with a drink in front of him. Their eyes met. Joe flicked his head to a high-sided booth. When they were seated, Harry said, "How you doing, Joe?" His voice was friendly.

"Yah, I'm ok. What are you drinking?" He signaled the waitress.

"Beer," Harry replied.

After their drinks were on the table, Kurtz continued, "I've got a small job for you, if you're interested."

Harry smiled and nodded. "Yeah, that's great. I could sure use a couple of bucks."

"This job will pay you $25.00. That's big money for what I've got in mind. There's a package I want you to deliver to Westerly, Rhode Island. I've written the address down. Do you think you can handle that?" Joe laid the paper on the table between them, but did not take his hand from it. "You'll leave tonight."

"Sure thing," Harry said. He sipped from his beer before adding, "But could I get a few bucks up front. I've got to gas up. With the price is up to twenty-eight cents a gallon, I'll need some front money."

Joe gave a short laugh and put a five-dollar bill on top of the directions. He slid the paper across the table. "You'll get the other half when you get back." He lifted his hand, put two fingers up as a signal to the barkeep before continuing the conversation. "I would do the run myself, but I've got more pressing business to take care of."

A second beer for Harry and another whiskey for Joe appeared. When the shot glass was empty Kurtz put his teeth together and sucked in his breath like the liquid was on fire. "After it's delivered, you are to call the number written on the bottom of the paper." Kurtz slid his eyes over the new employee. "No need to mention any names, just say the package has been delivered. That's all, understand?"

"Sure, simple, easiest money I've ever made." Harry put a smile on his face. He finished the beer in one long drink then wiped the froth from his upper lip with his shirtsleeve. "Consider it done."

The two men went around the corner to Joe's car. The gangster took a package the size of a shoebox from the front seat, passenger side. "Careful with this," he said.

"Why, what's in it, dynamite?" Harry chuckled.

"You're paid to deliver, no questions asked. Got it?" When Harry nodded, Kurtz handed him the box. It was wrapped in brown paper and tied tightly with string. "You know the way, right?"

"Yeah I can find it. I've been to Westerly before and I got a road map in the glove compartment of Rhode Island. With the directions you wrote on the paper it'll be a piece of cake. I'll be back before morning." They said goodbye. Harry headed for his car, thinking he'd better give Shiff a call from the road, but not until he was well clear of Kurtz.

Harry watched his rearview mirror for over an hour before stopping. When he was sure he wasn't being followed, he pulled into a gas station on the other side of the Cape Cod Canal. He was lucky to find one open that had a payphone inside. He dialed direct, watching through the window as the attendant put gas in the car and cleaned the windshield.

Harry explained the situation to his boss. Shiff called the shots. "I'd love to know what's in the box, but this could be a trap." Shiff told him to deliver the box unopened, exactly as it was wrapped. "Don't touch a thing. I want you to do whatever they ask, within reason of course."

Shiff was talking fast. "Call me if you can. Try not to let too much time go by without being in touch. Call your uncle in Provincetown and leave a message. Got it?" Detective Shiff knew that Harry would play his part. "As my old man would say, *stay safe, warm and dry.*"

"That's the second time someone said that to me tonight," Harry said while putting the receiver back into its cradle on the wall.

Chapter 19

The next morning Chief Crowley was at his desk staring at the corkboard. He didn't like to think that he might have to reveal what was going on between Mildred Kurtz and Billy, but if he had too, he would. The chief wrote the name Adams on a card and tacked it to the board. For the time being the card would remain blank. The cards across the board were beginning to hold details, but still not enough to tie anyone to the murder.

The chief went back to his desk to tackle the work that was waiting for him. There were budget sheets from the Board of Selectman that needed to be looked over. He was working on a request for part-time summer help. Crowley would also talk to the Board about the fishermen's request to use the town hall for a dance. He would talk to the Board about the traffic proposal that he would like to see in place before the tourist season. Parking was an issue that Mrs. Garrison had brought to light. He laid his pen down and stared off into space.

Crowley was alone in the office because Lewis was taking back the hours he'd spent watching the Kurtz's house. The chief looked at the pile of papers on his desk and sighed.

When the phone rang the chief answered after one ring. It was Shiff. "How's it going, James?" The Boston detective didn't wait for an answer. He continued, "I'll be coming your way this week. Can you spare me some of your precious time?"

"Maybe you should be spending more of your precious time in Boston rather than vacationing in Provincetown," came the response. Crowley thought of the conversation he'd had with Harry the previous night. "Joking aside, how is our mutual friend doing? Any word?"

"As a matter of fact things are progressing nicely. He picked up his first job and it went smoothly. I'm hoping this will lead to bigger and better things for the lad, but that's not why I wanted to see you." The Boston Detective had been busy. "I'll fill you in when I get there." Shiff's rapid speech slowed as he continued, "I know the walls have ears down your way. Things might be innocently said and repeated, causing all kinds of mischief and mayhem. I'll be in your office by nine, Monday morning. See you then." He hung up.

Crowley tried to concentrate on the sheets for his budget and the other items needing his attention. A wave of relief passed over him when the phone rang again. "Crowley speaking."

"Chief I need you to get over here and do something about these damn birds. The crows are frightening all my chickadees." The woman on the other end was a thorn in the chief's side, but he liked her. She called at least once a month with the most bizarre requests. Last month she saw a peeping Tom and wanted the chief to conduct a search of her property.

He listened patiently then said, "Mrs. Monroe, there is nothing I can do to stop the birds from chasing each other. It's part of nature."

She didn't like his explanation and ignored it. "Bring your gun. That should do it. Just a few shots and I think the crows will leave."

"So will the chickadees, Mrs. Monroe." At this point the woman was silent and the chief thought he would rather talk about the birds than work on the budget.

"Oh, well, maybe you can think of something else to keep them away," the wavering voice said. "But I think you should check it out. Your official, maybe you have some ideas."

"Try a scarecrow. It worked for John Silva and his cornfield. I can't come over there right now. I'm busy. But I'll stop by as soon as I can." The chief didn't like putting the old woman off, so he waited for Mrs. Monroe to say good-bye. Instead he heard an audible hissing sound, then a snort, and then silence. "I'm fixing clam chowder for lunch," she said. The chief was going to tell her he couldn't come, but she had already hung up.

James considered how easy his job was before murder came to town. Mrs. Monroe made him smile. He would most likely go to see the old woman and have a cup of chowder with her. It was really all she wanted, just a bit of company.

He took a ride to see the old woman, then he did his tour through the town. It was filling with happy strangers, vendors and smiling faces of locals as he waved to those he knew.

The chief was back in the office by one o'clock and was ready to leave at three. He told the operator where he would be. "I'll be out this evening at the Provincetown Inn until eleven, and then home. Call Sergeant Lewis if we have an emergency." The chief gave her Lewis's phone number, although she probably knew it by heart. It was easier to let the town's switchboard operator know where he'd be than to have her calling all over town looking for him.

He had very little in the way of a private life. Everyone would know by tomorrow that he had been out on a date with Susan. Tonight at the Provincetown Inn, Crowley and Susan would talk to shop-owners, bankers, fishermen, their wives and other citizens who liked to hear music and dance. There is no place to hide in a small town. He was hoping it would be the same for the murderer.

Crowley headed home. He took a hot shower, shaved, trimming his mustache, and dressed with care. His lightweight jacket with a clean handkerchief tucked into the pocket was hanging next to the door. He looked in the mirror and gave a small whistle, admiring what he saw.

Even in this lighthearted mood he thought constantly of the case. Earlier in the day the chief spoke with the neighbors on Nickerson and Bradford Streets. He asked if anyone had seen anything unusual on Monday or Tuesday night. Perhaps Frank

White was picked up in another car after he'd parked his near the edge of town. Maybe he'd get lucky and add something new to the investigation. No one noticed anything unusual.

Meanwhile there was tonight. He put on his jacket and headed out the door. He had a surprise for Susan. He didn't want to see a movie. He didn't want to sit facing a screen. He wanted to look at her. A band would start playing at eight o'clock at the Provincetown Inn. They could have dinner and stay to listen to the music. James was hoping that she would like the idea and agree to change plans. Maybe he'd get to dance a slow one with her.

When she opened the door he became anxious about her reaction. "You look beautiful," he said. She wore a peach colored dress made of crepe that swirled around her legs. "I hope you don't mind," Crowley blurted out, "but I made reservations at the Provincetown Inn for supper. I was hoping we could stay for the dancing instead of going to the movie." He waited a second, no response came so he said, "I thought it would be fun."

She looked surprised, then smiled. "That sounds wonderful. But am I dressed right for that. Doesn't everyone wear formal to those dances?"

"Well yes, no, sometimes," he stuttered. "The ladies dress in all kinds of clothing when they go there to dance, especially when they have a big band playing. Evening gowns to plain skirts. It doesn't matter as long as you're enjoying the music. I think you look just right." He meant every word.

They talked about their lives all evening. She asked many questions and seemed interested in everything he said. They sat at a table away from the dance floor so that they could hear each other. He told her about his budget problems and they laughed about some of the daily problems in a small town, like the overturned cart on Commercial Street last summer that spilled Jimmy Peet's strawberries onto the road. Everyone filled their pockets to keep them from getting stepped on. A few were eaten on the spot and some went home in pockets. It made the chief aware that he needed to work on speeding laws. It had been a speeding vehicle that upset the cart.

James asked how Ms. Alter was doing. Susan said she was fine and that led to her asking about the investigation. "We are just beginning to pull the investigation into a bundle," James said. "I've got some good help, and things are progressing."

She casually remarked, "Cherchez la femme."

"Does that mean look for the woman?" He asked. "Because I'm looking at a beautiful one right now." She blushed and looked at her plate, then across the room and smiled

"Thank you," she said.

He turned the conversation to a more comfortable subject, Mrs. Monroe and her crows. Susan had tears of laughter in her eyes when the chief finished his account of the phone conversation.

James Crowley had grown up in Provincetown and was happy to share some of his favorite stories. "This town has a number of characters. Do you know the boat *Elmer S*?" he asked. When she shook her head. He told her about how the fishermen had nicknames for each other. "Last year the fishermen made a booklet that they gave away to ticket holders at the Fishermen's Ball. Crowley continued with the story, "The *Elmer S* was voted the most colorful boat in the fleet. It's painted red, white, blue, gray, pink, yellow, orange, purple and two other colors that have no names." She laughed out loud.

He mentioned some of the nicknames the fishermen had for each other: Romeo, The big Bad Wolf, Henry the Eighth, The Perfect Specimen, Professor Quiz, The Voice of Experience, Daddy's Boy, Gone With the Wind, The Face in the Fog, The Eyes and Ears of the World, The Jitterbugger, Rip Van Winkle and many others. "They know each other's nicknames," the chief said.

"And that's just a few of the names." James was enjoying

himself for the first time in days. "I think everyone in town has a nickname."

"How about you?" Susan asked.

"It depends on who you talk to. I'm sometimes called Duke, but I don't know why. I've been called some rotten names over the years, mostly when I'm locking someone up, but they don't count. Around Provincetown, people call me Chief," Crowley said.

When Susan told him she would return to Boston in August to teach, Crowley said he couldn't think that far into the future, but he was nevertheless unhappy at the prospect. There were sighs when he took her home at eleven-thirty. Her cheeks were flushed and her eyes sparkled. She thanked him and held out her hand for him to shake. He took it in his and held it while he asked, "Can I call on you again?"

"I think that would be fine." She looked into his dark brown eyes and knew there was more to know about this man.

He didn't let go of her hand, instead pulled her close and kissed her, lightly on the mouth, just brushing her lips and then pressing, covering her mouth. He wanted more, but he would not ruin this evening by doing or saying something he might regret. They pulled apart. She smiled and said, "Good night, Duke."

Chapter 20

Sunday was quiet. The chief checked with the operator for missed calls. There were none. He ate at Betty's, went to Saint Mary's Church and then took a ride through town. Monday morning spread across the bay bringing the temperature to sixty-five by seven o'clock. Crowley was seated at his desk when the phone rang. "Crowley speaking."

It was Doc Rice. "Are you going to be in for the next half hour? I thought I'd stop by on my way to the office, but I didn't want to waste my time if you were home sleeping off the dancing." The doctor laughed. "I'll be right over." He hung up without letting the chief say a word.

Dr. Rice had his black bag in his hand when he came through the office door. "Beautiful morning. I understand you had a good time on Saturday night." The doctor waited for the chief to give him grief for being teased, but the chief just smiled.

"I knew everyone in town would have me marrying the girl by next week." Crowley's ears turned pink and he added, "My, how word gets around. Too bad we can't find the murderer that quick, then we could all go on vacation." Chief Crowley's rugged face showed lines at the outside of his eyes when he smiled. "Yes I had a good time. First date, not serious, now can we move on?" He paused, "What brings you here so early in the day?"

"Might be early for you, but I've been up all night with Mrs. Oliver. How come so many children are born at night, do you ever wonder about that?" The doctor placed his black bag on the chief's desk and continued without waiting for an answer. "I think I may know what the weapon is. When I was at the Oliver home last night, delivering a healthy baby boy, by the way, I happened to see a pair of pinking shears, those big sewing scissors. I think they're called shears. My wife has a pair. Anyway, the husband thought I was a bit daft when I asked if I could borrow them for a couple of days." Rice opened his bag and pulled out a large pair of scissors and put them on Crowley's desk. "What do you think?"

Both men looked at the instrument. They appeared to be about twelve inches long with black handles. The pair had thick blades with sharp edges that fit together with precision.

The chief spoke first. "They'll have to be measured and compared to the wound?" The chief tried not to appear excited. He continued, "I'll give the County ME a call, ask him take a look, see what he thinks. They can do the measuring while they have the body." Crowley stood up and went around the desk. "Thanks doc. Let's hope they fill the bill."

Doctor Rice picked up the scissors as if weighing them in his hand. "I'll need to return these to Mrs. Oliver when you're done with them." Dr. Rice said. "With the new baby she'll be doing more sewing. Her husband said they didn't come cheap. You should be able to find a similar pair here in town, try the New York Store."

The doctor looked like he was falling asleep, eyelids closed, hands on belly, and deep breaths. When he opened his eyes he continued where he left off. "They're fairly common, so I don't know if it's going to help your investigation much," Doctor Rice said. "I'll leave you to sort out the technical problems."

Crowley took the scissors from the doc. "If they turn out to be what we are looking for, I'll buy the new baby a gift." Both men had smiles on their faces. The chief added, "I'll head over to the New York Store and get a new pair. You can return these to Mrs. Oliver tomorrow. Thanks Doc."

"Anytime I can give you a hand it warms the cockles of my heart. Now tell me about this young lady you were whirling around the dance floor the other evening." The man waited for Crowley to spill the beans.

Crinkles appeared at the edges of the chief's eyes. "You

don't know her and I'm not telling you a thing. You're probably the worst gossip in this town. My phone will be ringing off the hook and Mrs. Bateman will be wondering why I didn't ask her granddaughter from Harvard out dancing. I have enough trouble without you starting more. Now try to concentrate on murder and leave my love life out of it."

The chief shook his index finger at his friend. "I'd be very grateful if you don't mention the scissors or my date to anyone."

"You know me better than that." Doctor Rice said. They left it at that. It appeared the subject of the woman was off limits for the time being.

Crowley asked about his son and was told he'd be leaving in two weeks for North Carolina. There was a lament in his voice and the creases in his puffy face seemed to deepen. "My wife is counting the days." He shook his head.

Crowley placed the scissors in a large brown envelope. He picked up his hat, tucked the envelope under his arm, and along with the doctor, left the office. Lewis was at the front desk. He told the patrolman where he was going, adding, "I have something that will require overtime for you this afternoon. We'll talk when I get back."

The sun was high as the two men shook hands before going their separate ways. Doc Rice went toward his car, a 1936 Hudson that was parked at the rear of the town hall. Crowley headed in the opposite direction. Commercial Street was quiet. Johnny Mott's pool hall was closed. Work was being done to the front exterior of Seamen's Bank. It looked like new clapboard siding. Crowley walked around the ladders and scaffolding. He said good morning to the carpenters and hurried along the street, taking deep breaths of fresh air as he went.

A bell over the door tinkled as the chief stepped over the threshold. Seated on a stool behind a glass counter was a woman whose name the chief could not remember. She had an apron over

her dress and her hair was pulled up and tied with a bright yellow ribbon. She was filing her nails. She looked up and smiled. "Hi, Chief Crowley. Can I help you?"

"Yes, I'm looking for scissors, big ones, the kind that cuts heavy material." Crowley opened the envelope. "Like these," he said. He showed her what he was looking for.

The woman put the nail file down on the shelf of the cash register. "Back this way. They'll be with our sewing supplies." The chief followed her through the store, passing shelves filled with kitchen utensils, rolling pins, measuring cups, dishes, nutcrackers, and many other items that Crowley didn't recognize. The aisles were neatly arranged in rows and filled with every conceivable thing required to keep a home well stocked.

Rolls of brightly colored cloth hung on slender metal rods along the back wall. The fabric could be pulled off at the desired length and then cut. Crowley glanced at dress patterns, spools of thread, needles, skeins of wool for knitting along with other sewing utensils. A locked display case in the corner held the scissors. They were arranged by size from the smallest used for cutting baby's fingernails to the largest that appeared to be twelve inches long. Crowley pointed to the largest pair with oval shaped handles. They felt heavy in his grip. "I'll take them," he said.

The counter girl asked, "Would you like me to wrap them for you?"

The chief nodded. "Thank you."

On the way back to the register Crowley asked, "Do you happen to keep a record of who else might have purchased this kind of scissor?"

The girl shook her head, "No we don't write down names of people. People usually pay cash, but sometimes it goes into a store credit. Sometimes people buy things and then pay for them at the end of the month, that's if the boss has approved their credit. Plus we've been selling that kind of scissor for years."

The chief thanked her again. He placed the receipt in the bag and left.

As soon as he was back at his desk he called the county Medical Examiner's Office and spoke to a secretary who told him that the doctor would call him back at noon. Crowley looked at the clock. He had to wait. He picked up the phone again and asked the operator for 1394.

A few moments later he was talking to Susan, "Hello James, so nice of you to call. I had a wonderful time Saturday night."

"Good, me too. I was hoping we could maybe catch that movie you wanted to see, maybe sometime this week." He waited and realized he was holding his breath.

"I think that particular movie is gone, but I'll see what else is playing. How about Thursday?" She answered. They agreed on a time to pick her up. Both said goodbye at the same time. She laughed and hung up.

Crowley was smiling when picked up his pipe from the holder on the desk. He didn't light it. He wasn't sure where the scissors, his relationship, or the case was going, but plans were taking shape. Somewhere in the back of his mind he had a clearer picture of what he was looking for.

At noon he spoke to the doctor at the Medical Examiner's Office, in Pocasset. Crowley explained what had been discovered and asked if he could send the scissors to have a comparison made with the wound. The medical examiner said he was glad to help. He said, "I'll get to it as soon as they arrive." Crowley thanked the doctor and hung up.

The chief hollered down the hall, his voice echoing against the cement walls, "Lewis, can you come in here? And bring coffee." He added, "Please."

Lewis arrived carrying two cups in his hand. He placed them on the desk, and sat down. "What's up?" the policeman asked.

"I've got a job for you," the chief said. He placed the scissors in front of Lewis. "Doc Rice brought these to me this morning. I bought an identical pair at the New York Store while I was out. I'd like you to take them to the Barnstable County Medical Examiner's Office today." Crowley explained about using them for comparison. "Even if we don't have the exact weapon a positive comparison will move us in the right direction. Can you go to Pocasset today?"

Lewis nodded. His head bounced as if it were attached to a spring, while he listened to what the chief had to say. "Do you know the way?" the chief asked.

Lewis replied, "I've been there before. I drove Mrs. Viagas after her husband's body was found. You remember he was drowned when his fishing boat sank and his body washed up on Lieutenants Island. I drove her to the county morgue to identify his remains. That was a trip I'll never forget. She cried all the way there and back. Sad, so sad, hope I never have to do that again."

"I remember," the chief said. They talked about the tragedy and the difficult lives the fishermen faced each day. For a moment they were silent, and then Lewis said, "I'd better get going."

"Take your time. County Road is busy this time of the year. Get some lunch before you leave. You should be able to make the trip to Pocasset and back in time for supper." The chief looked at the budget sheets on his desk. "Don't bother coming back into the office. Take the car home and give me a call when you're back." Lewis said that would be fine and left Crowley sitting at his desk, looking at the murder board.

Chapter 21

Billy Adams and Ernie Thomas bent over a pile of fish that was dropped from the net onto the deck of the *Sea Crest*. The boat moved in a wide circle, towing the net slowly through the water. They were on the Middle Bank, seven miles north of Race Point Light. They picked up a variety of fish: skates, yellow tail flounder, black-back flounder, dabs, and five hundred pounds of codfish and a couple of lobsters. The fish in the wire baskets were washed with the deck hose and dumped into wooden boxes. The one hundred pound boxes were then wrestled into the fish-hole. The crewman stacked them in the pens below deck.

When all the saleable fish was stowed, they pushed whatever was left off the deck, through the scuppers, and back into the sea. They could not sell monkfish. No one would eat sea cucumbers, believing them to be inedible. They shoved broken bottles filled with sand, cow-tale a useless sponge-like bottom vegetation, a couple of dog-fish that would appear by the thousands in the summer, and countless crabs that no one wanted, back where they came from. The lobsters were sold for cash at local restaurants and the fish to Atlantic Coast Fisheries.

Billy tied a particular type of knot at bottom of the net. He looped a rolling hitch, around and around. It would hold the net closed and could be pulled apart with a few tugs. The two men maneuvered the heavy wet twine over the side. Billy went to the wheelhouse and turned the wheel to port. The boat moved forward. The net hung waiting to enter the water. Billy hollered, "Set out." The crewman lifted the brake that held the line and the net fell into the sea. The tow would last an hour and then the routine would begin again.

Ernie disappeared below deck into the galley to prepare a

lunch. Billy went to the wheelhouse to sit in his chair and stare out the window at the seemingly endless sea. He thought about how Millie was distracted and frightened the last time they saw each other. Her husband was at home more often lately and the front window was kept dark.

Billy was worried. Millie told him that she was afraid of Joe. She said he spoke about how our country was on the path to destruction and ruin. Lately he was saying things that she didn't understand about how he felt the government should work, about political unrest, and demonstrations. "Other countries are solving their problems with strong leadership," her husband had told her.

Billy felt his chest tighten. He felt sure that the situation was becoming urgent. He thought about running away, leaving his home, the town, and his fishing business. His thoughts were a jumble. They would need money. They would need to go where her husband couldn't find them. Where would they go? He was sure he would find a way out, for both their sakes.

The fisherman didn't usually pay attention to gossip, but when his crewman told him that a dead man was brought into Richland's funeral parlor last Wednesday, Billy listened. "The police are keeping it a secret," he said. "Don't ask me why, but you know how small towns are. You spit on one side of town and in ten minutes it's known on the other." Billy was thinking, wishing it were Millie's husband that had died.

The young captain shifted in his seat, adjusted the steering wheel, and thought about what his crewman had said. "However you slice it, a man is dead and I heard that the police think it may be murder."

Billy didn't give the chief the whole truth when Crowley appeared at his apartment. It was his sin of omission. It would look suspicious if he fled with Millie now. He wanted to have a life with the woman he loved. Her husband would never give her a divorce. They had discussed it. The lovers would wait, but a plan was taking shape.

The boat moved smoothly through the gray sea, rocking gently from side to side, soothing Billy's fears. He loved being out on the water. It was hard work and sometimes there was no catch or very little pay, but the incentive was always there. He was always hoping that the next tow would be a popper, a full net jumping to the top of the water as the codfish bladders expanded. The net would rise in the water and pop when it hit the surface. This had happened on a few occasions. It caused a rush of pride and adrenaline. It would mean a week's pay for the crew.

The captain stared out the small window. The sight of a shimmering sea brought thoughts of sparkling eyes, ruby mouth, and soft thick hair. The scent of the sea reminded him of her body. In the distance a large whale jumped out of the water. These creatures often surrounded the boats as they fished. The giants were mysterious. Billy's thoughts came to a sudden stop. He watched the splash and slap of water as the great leviathan crashed back into the deep. Sometimes the whales lay on top of the water as if sunning themselves or sleeping. The boat could get close enough to smell the exhaled breath coming from the blowholes, fouling the air with a rancid odor.

On occasion his boat came close enough to touch one of the beasts. He had heard stories of boats that were sunk in minutes after striking one. He wished there was some way of making money from the giant sea creatures. Hunting whales was long past. His grandfather had done well in the whaling business, but today no one wanted the meat, the blubber, or the oil. And so the whales and the fishing boats moved through the same water, never touching, but suspicious and curious of the other. Billy was thinking of how they both traveled upon the sea taking food as if it were God's plan that they should share the ocean's bounty.

As the sun descended into the western horizon, the captain

called his crewman onto the deck. "Let's haul back, clean up, and head in. I don't know about you, but I'm beat." He never used the Portuguese language that he'd grown up listening to, but there was a hint of it in his words that sounded like music. "We've had a good catch today, it's going to take a couple of hours to get in and then another to unload, we'll be lucky if we finish up before dark." The net was hauled in. Fish were dumped and the net left to hang in the mast to dry.

A feeling of accomplishment washed over the men as the lines were tied to the poles on the wharf. Billy was relaxed and tired. Captain and crew worked together to secure the boat. They spoke about going out again in the morning.

Tony said good night and walked away. He noticed a woman walking up the pier toward the icehouse. Tony nodded his head, thinking someone had come too late looking for a free fish. The crewman didn't stop, but Billy did. He was more than a little surprised to see Millie standing in the shadows.

"What are you doing here? It's late." He took her by the elbow and moved into the alley between the fish-house and the side of a fisherman's shed. "We can't let anyone see us together. It's not safe." The words came tumbling from Billy. He spoke rapidly, "Millie, you look cold." He wrapped his jacket around her thin yellow dress.

Millie grabbed his hands in both of hers. "Billy," was all she said. She looked down at her feet. She was wearing thin-soled, dainty shoes that appeared in direct contrast to the thick rubber boots that Billy wore. She looked at the wooden planks under her feet. A flash of memory came to her of a child walking with here mother and father across planks like these. Her father had stepped upon the railing of a schooner, waved goodbye, and left. He never returned. For Millie the wharf evoked the feeling of loss. Ironically, she had fallen in love with a fisherman.

She picked her head up and looked at her lover. "Crowley came to see me today. He asked me questions about Joe." Millie seemed as fragile as a butterfly.

He wanted to hold her. They moved further into the shadow of the building. "The night has eyes," he said. Then he pulled her close and kissed her.

She pushed him away. "Please Billy, not now. I'm worried. Crowley said things to me. He thinks Joe has something to do with Nazis." A shiver ran through her. "Nazis, I could hardly take in what he was talking about."

"Did he ask you about me?" Billy could see that tears were shimmering at the edges of Millie's eyes.

"Yes." Millie looked into her lover's eyes and said, "He said he knew all about our meetings. I almost threw up. But mostly he asked about Joe. I didn't tell him anything, because I really don't know what my husband does when he's gone. He asked specifically about Joe being home on Monday and Tuesday nights. And he asked if you'd come to see me on either of those nights." Tears were welling up in her eyes. Billy put his hand up to tenderly brush her cheek.

"What did you tell him?" Billy asked.

"I said that you didn't come to the house on either night, and I told him that Joe didn't come home until Wednesday. Is that ok?" She had her hand up against her mouth and looked like a child unsure of what was happening.

Billy took her hands and kissed them lightly. He said, "Chief Crowley came to see me as well. He knows all about us. He asked me about your husband as well. He's probably checking to see if our stories match. I'm sure it has to do with the dead man they found on the beach. Your husband is a suspect."

Millie continued, "I'm so confused and I'm frightened. I can't even think straight. Billy, a man came to the house on Thursday. He was angry with Joe. They were arguing and Joe looked scared to death. I didn't tell Chief Crowley about him. Should I say something? Billy?"

"I think we should tell the chief about it. Leave it to me. I'll call him." Billy wanted to give Crowley something that would take the spotlight from them and put it on Joe Kurtz.

Billy ran his hand through his hair. "Crowley thinks that your husband is involved with some bad people." Billy was slow to add, "I think he's suspects him of being a part to the Nazi Party." Billy swayed slightly as if still on the deck of the boat. "We need to stay apart for awhile.

"Stay quiet, do as your husband asks, and don't say anything to anyone." He whispered in her ear, "It will be alright, Mil. I love you." Their kiss was deep and long while they listened to the sound of distant surf as it rolled onto the land, scratching and hissing, the sound that came with low tide. "I love you," he repeated. I'll find a way out for us."

Chapter 22

It was the sixth time in three days that Harry drove his '33 Ford along County Road. Driving gave him time to think. He was anxious and wanted something to happen and that put dangerous ideas in his head. It was past midnight when he drove into the parking area in front of the redesigned barn. He cut the engine and turned off the headlights.

Harry waited. If anyone asked questions, he had a ready answer. No one came snooping. There was no sign of life in the house or barn, no lights, and no cars parked in the yard. After fifteen minutes he slipped from the car and went to the barn's side entrance. He tried the door. It was locked.

Carefully he made his way around to the back of the building and found a window. With a little effort he was able to push it open and squeeze his body through. He fell onto a dirt floor. Using a Zippo lighter for light he looked around. He was in an old stall. Lifting the latch on the door, he stepped into an office. The glow from the Zippo cast a dim light on a desk, filing cabinet and boxes piled along one wall.

Harry went to the desk and switched on a hooded lamp. He opened one drawer after the next, closing each one with care. He worked quickly. The file cabinet next to the desk was a standard grey metal similar to the one used at his office in Boston. The top drawer contained files with names that he didn't recognize. He slipped one out and opened it. It was a ledger with numbers written in columns. Bookkeeping was not something he was familiar with. As he replaced the file he wondered how this could help the investigation.

The second drawer contained more file folders with names written on them, many he recognized from newspaper accounts.

One stood out, Charles A. Lindbergh. The file contained newspaper articles about the famous pilot and his famous first flight across the Atlantic in his plane the *Spirit of St. Lewis*. Harry remembered reading about the famous aviator's recent trips to Germany and his meetings with Herr Hitler. Lindbergh was known for his support of the America First Committee, whose agenda supported non-intervention, anti-war, and non-aggression, by the United States against any country including Germany.

America First believed that if Hitler were left alone he would get what he wanted and the war would end of it's own volition. The movement was popular in 1937-38 with over 800,000 members, but that was before Germany invaded Poland and then took Czechoslovakia.

Harry scanned photographs from a folder. One caught his attention, Hitler surrounded by his *brown shirts,* the *Strum Abteilung,* his storm troopers. This group began in the early 1930's with the purpose of protecting Hitler at Nazi meetings. It soon grew. They disrupted the meetings of his political rivals and had a reputation as a well-organized, violent gang of thugs. In 1933 they led a boycott of Jewish owned businesses in Germany. This gradually grew to include social, political and legal exclusion of Jews.

The America First Committee disbanded soon after news of *Kristallnacht,* night of the broken glass was made public. America came to see Germany's mission, it's totalitarian dictatorship, in a whole new light. During *Kristallnacht* the windows of Jewish owned stores, homes, synagogues, and schools were destroyed, leaving broken glass scattered on every street. It is believed that thirty thousand Jewish men disappeared that night, taken to work camps. Hitler had begun his systematic *Final Solution* to what he called the *Jewish Problem*.

Charles Lindberg spoke in favor of Germany's politics and had won over countless persons who supported non-intervention in the European war. America First called upon President Roosevelt to keep America out of the European war.

Harry understood their point of view. He wanted peace as much as the next person, but to him, freedom was the issue. Heir Hitler had repeated over and over that Germany would become a leading nation with a superior race of men and women. Harry knew there was no freedom left in Germany.

He put the folder back in its place and scanned through the others. Another name caught his attention, Frank White. The file contained dates, places (presumably of deliveries) and the amount paid. The entries ended a week before his body was discovered in Provincetown. Harry slipped the cardboard folder back into place and closed the drawer.

He climbed quickly out the window, closed it, and turned back toward the front of the barn. He brushed off his clothing and walked back the way he came. He was crossing the parking lot when headlights from a vehicle swept the area. The door to a Dodge pickup truck opened and Eddie the Enforcer stepped out.

"Hey!" He yelled out. "What are you doing there?" His voice matched the outline shadow of his frame, meaty, heavy, and solid. He was rapidly moving toward Harry as he shouted, "I said, what are you doing?"

Harry put his hands up, palms out. He called out, "It's me Harry Enos. I was just taking a leak." He turned toward the side of the barn. Harry pulled at the zipper of his pants and walked slowly toward the square bulk of the man. Eddie seemed to plant his feet in the ground. Harry could see the pistol in his hand.

His voice echoed across the quiet night. "Come here. And keep your hands where I can see them," Eddie hollered.

The two men stood four feet apart, facing each other. The enforcer seemed to relax somewhat when he recognized Harry. "People have been hurt by being where they shouldn't be. Vat you doing here? There's no meeting tonight." Eddie didn't put the gun away just let his arm hang down.

Harry was prepared. "I stopped to get some rest. I've been driving nonstop. I needed a place I could pull over without some cop stopping by and asking questions like you are." Harry waited for the big man to reply. He didn't. So Harry added, "Now if it's ok with you, I've got to get back to Provincetown. Joe will be waiting to hear from me."

Eddie didn't like new members joining their group. For that matter, he didn't like people. He grunted, and then put the gun into his jacket pocket. The enforcer stepped aside. Harry passed without any words spoken. Eddie didn't take his eyes off of Harry until the car pulled out of the driveway.

Harry's heart was beating like a drum when he stepped on the gas pedal and headed for the tip of Cape Cod. He began to relax as he passed through Eastham. Twenty-five miles to go before he could stop, eat, and call Shiff.

Harry planned to use the phone at Crowley's house, but after his run-in with Eddie, he decided to call from a phone box along the way. He was certain that Eddie would let his boss know about the encounter.

From what Harry had seen in the files, this group was larger than they expected. The ledger noted large amounts of money. Shiff needed to know about it. The names of famous American's wouldn't go over well with those in Boston, but Shiff and Crowley would appreciate the information that White worked for these guys and was paid handsomely. There was now a definite link between this gang and the murdered man.

Eddie was capable of things that Harry didn't want to think about. It didn't take much to make the leap that the enforcer had something to do with White and maybe his death.

Harry made sure he wasn't followed and stopped at the General Store in Eastham to use the phone. It was a good place to call from because the booth couldn't be seen from the road. He dropped a dime into the coin slot and dialed the number he had memorized. His boss answered.

"I thought I'd pass along some news." Harry told Shiff what he'd discovered in the file cabinet and about his run-in with Eddie at the barn. "He'll let his boss know about finding me at the barn. I had a good excuse. My being there won't be a problem."

Shiff didn't like what he was hearing. "Listen Harry, be careful. These people are dangerous. This news about White working with them will give Crowley something to chew on. Is there any news on Joe Kurtz and his group of Brown Shirts?"

Harry brought his boss up to date. "I'm meeting with him tomorrow night at the Governor Bradford. He said something about a different job. I won't be able to call, so don't worry if you don't hear from me." He laughed a little. "Joe likes me," Harry said. "I'll be in touch."

Charles Shiff hated sending any of his officers into the eye of the storm, undercover, but it was the only way to know what this particular group of Nazi sympathizers was up to. It wasn't against the law to hold meetings, or talk about how they would like to see the government run. It wasn't against the law to support another political party. And as far as he knew they hadn't committed any crimes.

Terrorist acts, explosions in factories, an attempted bombing at a Naval Shipyard in Portsmouth, New Hampshire, and violent protest marches in large cities across America had taken place in the past year. Arrests had been made. It was always the small fry who were caught up in protesting, not the organizers and leaders. This group on the cape could give the government boys just what they wanted, inside information.

Socialist Party members, radical Bolsheviks, and other groups known for violent actions including the Third Reich, were under surveillance by the FBI. It was thought that these organizations provoked unrest by distributing anti-war propaganda. They preached collaboration with Germany, over throwing Russia, and changes in the political structure of the United States.

Shiff trusted Harry. Harry had saved his life. There had been a robbery at a fish dealer's office where a man was taken hostage. The thief wanted the cops to let him pass with the hostage. Shiff stepped into the street, raised his gun, and told the thief to surrender.

The robber fired, the hostage fainted and a bullet grazed Shiff's head. He had felt the disturbance in the air as the bullet whizzed passed. Harry saved the day. He came up behind the thief and slugged him with a truncheon. The man went down like a sack of potatoes, right on top of the hostage. Harry would take no credit, insisting he was only doing his job.

The phone call from Harry was severed after one minute. Shiff then picked up the phone and dialed the Provincetown exchange. The operator put him through to Crowley at home. "It's me," he said in a gruff voice without giving his name.

Shiff got right to the point. "I've heard from my nephew. He will be in your neck of the woods and I'm hoping you can keep an eye on him for me. Kids these days." Crowley understood the message. "He'll get in touch with you." Shiff could be heard taking a drag of the cigarette that Crowley imagined hanging from his mouth.

"He gave me some news about John Doe. He works with Mr. K. Looks like a big company, plenty of money. I understand Provincetown is lovely this time of year. I'll see you soon." The phone went dead before Crowley had a chance to say a word.

"Same old goat," the chief said as he put the phone back in its cradle.

Crowley went back to reading the weekly newspaper, *The Advocate*. There was an article that caught his attention. The caption read, "Mystery Surrounds Death." It said that a body had been found, but that at press time, the chief of police was unavailable for comment. The name of the deceased and details of the death were being withheld until notification of the relatives. The article mentioned that the man was taken to the County Medical Examiner's Office and that the victim's car had been confiscated.

Crowley was fit-to-be-tied. No one from the paper had called his office to ask about the death. He wanted to know where the editor got his information. Doc Rice, Mr. Richland, Joe Duarte and Lewis had been asked to keep tightlipped on what was going on. He knew they would. He sighed, "Such is life in a small town. Everyone enjoys the gossip too much." He closed the paper and his eyes.

He was dozing when the ringing phone brought him back from dreaming. "Hello."

"Chief this is Billy Adams, I hope its ok to call you at home. The operator put me through."

"Sure it's ok. What can I do for you?" The chief sounded groggy from unfulfilled sleep.

"I wanted to tell you what Millie told me about a man that visited Joe last week. She said that this man and her husband had an argument. She didn't know what it was about, but her husband seemed nervous," Billy said.

"What was this man's name?" The chief asked.

"She heard, Eddie. She said he was a big man, built like a bull, solid, and scary." Billy tried to remember everything that Millie had told him.

"Could she hear what was being said?" Crowley questioned.

"Only parts of the conversation." Billy stopped. He needed to think. "I'm telling you so that you won't have to talk to Millie. She's worried." Billy hesitated then asked, "Chief, Millie's frightened. Please, Can you keep her out of this?"

"I'm going to have to talk to her, but I'll be discrete. I'll see her when her husband isn't around." Crowley said. The chief thanked him and then hung up. "Interesting," the policeman said to the empty room. He wouldn't push too hard, the woman was frightened, frail, and alone.

It had been a warm day, but that night the temperature dropped. He heard a rumble of thunder. Rain was coming, spreading its way across the bay, bringing with it relief to the parched sandy soil. The chief got up and closed the windows.

Chapter 23

The following morning Lewis sat facing Crowley across the desk. Both men were sipping coffee. They were discussing the article in the newspaper. "In the clear light of day," the chief said, "maybe this was just what the investigation needed. A sort of a call to action." Looking at the corkboard, Crowley added, "Let's get Mr. Kurtz into the office. I want you to go back to Nickerson Street while Mr. Kurtz is here. Get a look around the house. Talk to Mrs. Kurtz and be direct. Ask about her husband, his business dealings, names he may have mentioned, and especially Eddie who visited last week. Ask again if her husband was home on Monday and Tuesday nights."

The chief looked at the corkboard, then at his notebook. "Also ask her about our victim. Has her husband ever mentioned the name Frank White? Show her the picture of White." Crowley didn't like the idea of showing the fragile woman the post mortem photo, but he felt he had no choice.

"Skip her relationship with Billy," the chief continued, "I think we have all we need on that subject. We don't want to frighten her, so go gently. She may have information that she doesn't' know is important."

The chief began leafing through his notepad. He added, "I'll keep her husband here for at least half an hour, be in and out in that time frame. Use that nice watch your mom gave you for Christmas. Half an hour, that's it. That should give you time to ask a few questions, check out the house, and be gone before the husband leaves my office."

Crowley and Lewis discussed Shiff's project, the undercover agent, and the terror known as the Brown Shirts. The chief explained that Frank White was working with Joe Kurtz's group out of Orleans. "They're a dangerous gang. We need to tread lightly when talking to both Mildred and Joe Kurtz. There must be no mention of Harry at any time, understood?"

The coffee grew cold. "Pick up Mr. Kurtz and bring him here. Tell him I'd like to ask him a couple of questions. Say we are talking to everyone in the neighborhood. Say that it's a courtesy call." Lewis nodded. "Do not mention Nazis, Frank White or anything to do with the case. Tell him that all his questions will be answered when he gets here."

Lewis stood up and looked at the clock on the wall. It was just before noon. "I'll take that ride up Nickerson."

The chief shooed his sergeant out by flicking his fingers as the phone began to ring. He picked up the receiver and said, "Crowley here."

After introducing himself as the County Medical Examiner, Dr. Morris said. "I have some interesting news for you. You did a good job with identifying the murder weapon. The scissors that you sent me match the wound on Mr. White's body, quite precisely. That particular pair has no trace of blood and was not used in the murder, but the weapon you are looking for is very similar in length, width and shape. I'll send you a written report with a bit more technical details. I hope that helps."

Chief Crowley thanked the doctor and hung up the phone. He pulled open the top drawer of his desk and lifted the scissors belonging to Mrs. Oliver. He laid them on the desk, in front of his phone in plain view. The chief then went to the murder board and turned it to face the wall.

It was twelve-fifteen when a tap on Crowley's office door. Lewis followed Joe Kurtz into the small office. The man that stood in front of him looked decades older than his wife. A fleeting picture of Billy Adams crossed Crowley's mind. He offered his hand. The other man did not take it. "Thank you for coming in.

Have a seat Mr. Kurtz," the chief said. "Sargent Lewis, you can go, thank you." Lewis nodded and left the two men alone.

Kurtz did not sit. "What's this all about, chief?" He removed his hat and wiped the sheen of sweat from his forehead with a handkerchief. He then replaced the spotless white cloth, patting the pocket afterward. He had on a lightweight, pinstriped suit over a white shirt. His hair was slicked back, thinning, and gave off an odor of spice.

"We are talking to everyone who lives in the vicinity of Nickerson Street and Bradford Street. It's a quiet neighborhood and we're hoping someone will remember seeing something out of the ordinary last Monday or Tuesday." This had the effect Crowley was hoping for. Kurtz blinked and straightened his shoulders. The chief continued, "Please have a seat."

Joe Kurtz sat down in the chair. His body was rigid.

"An automobile was abandoned in the area and we are looking for the owner," Crowley explained.

Kurtz relaxed, his shoulders dropped slightly, and he looked directly at the chief. "I travel a great deal in my work for the Fuller Company and I was not at home on Monday or Tuesday. So I'm afraid I can't help you." The salesman said.

The atmosphere became charged when the chief asked, "Perhaps you can tell me if the name Frank White means anything to you?"

Kurtz narrowed his eyebrows. He shifted in his seat, but did not answer. The white handkerchief came out of the jacket pocket and Kurtz looked at it while he fished for an answer. "I don't know the name, but then I meet so many people in my line of work." Joe Kurtz hesitated, paused, and finally said, "I didn't see anything out of the ordinary on Monday, Tuesday, or any other day. I told you, I wasn't home. Is there a problem?"

"We have an eye witness that saw you take something from the vehicle owned by Mr. White last Wednesday evening. A good neighbor with a watchful eye." Crowley waited. He listened to the clock ticking. Mr. Kurtz shifted in his chair, unbuttoned his jacket, and then adjusted the white handkerchief that he placed back in the left breast pocket. The chief continued, "So let's begin again. How do you know Mr. White?"

Kurtz's eyes wandered around the room, stopping at the murder board that had been turned to face the wall. He began slowly, "Mr. White was supposed to deliver a box of supplies to my home. I saw his car," he hesitated, "And had a look. The box was sitting on the front seat." Kurtz let out a breath, looked at Chief Crowley, and smiled with lips only. "OK? Like I said that box belonged to me."

He slowed his words and spoke in a soft voice. "Mr. White has a delivery service that I use occasionally. He works for many people. I mean he makes deliveries for different people." He stopped talking, brushed a thread from the lapel of his jacket. "Why are you asking? I didn't steal it if that's what you think."

Crowley was soft spoken, making an effort not to raise his voice. He did not want to give away any information about the investigation. The man looked at the chief as if waiting for an explanation. "A man is dead," the chief paused. "You were seen at his car. That makes me wonder how well you knew the man. You knew his car when you saw it and you admit to knowing the dead man."

Joe Kurtz's reaction was swift. His eyes opened wide. There was surprise in his voice. "You mean Frank White is dead?"

Joe Kurtz was looking at the scissors on Crowley's desk. He spoke while raising his eyes to the wall in back of Crowley's desk. "I hardly knew the man. He sometimes made deliveries for me, runs errands for some business acquaintances. I needed the supplies for work, for our next business meeting. That's all." Joe Kurtz was now the legitimate businessman. " I'm sorry to hear he's dead. What happened?" Kurtz asked.

"Didn't you see last night's *Advocate*? It's been all over the news." Kurtz shook his head no. Crowley continued, "The article didn't mention a name because we are waiting to notify relatives. Perhaps you can help us with that since you knew the man."

The salesman again shook his head, "I don't know much about him, really. He lives in Gloucester, I think. I met him a couple of times. I'm sorry to hear about his demise, but I can't help you. "

"So tell me," Crowley leaned back in his chair. "Do you know why his car was parked on Bradford Street?" The room was silent. Kurtz had his head tilted and was looking at the closet door.

"I don't know," the salesman said.

"Why didn't you wait for him to deliver the box?" Crowley asked as Joe Kurtz began to readjust his position. The Chief continued, "Where did you think he was?"

"I was on my way home. I thought it looked like his car. I wasn't sure at first. I went to my home first then walked back to see if was Mr. White's car. I just had a look inside and saw the box from my company. He wasn't around so I thought I'd save him some time on his route. That's it. That's all I know." Joe Kurtz lifted his chin and sat up straighter in the chair.

Crowley asked, "What was so important that you had to sneak out at night to get the box?" He could see the other man's jaw tighten.

Joe Kurtz became indignant. "I wasn't sneaking. It was late when I got home. The supplies are for my business. I told you. I needed them for my deliveries in the morning, for my business. I had no idea where the man was, I don't keep track of him." The chief had seen the pamphlets. They had nothing to do with the Fuller Brush Company. Crowley didn't mention the contents of the box.

"Where were you last week, Monday and Tuesday?" Chief Crowley asked.

"Do I need an alibi?" Again Kurtz took the hankie out of

his breast pocket and wiped his upper lip. When the chief did not answer, Joe continued, "I was out of town, with business associates." Mr. Kurtz set his mouth in a grim smirk. "Now if you have no further questions, I have other things to do today, or are you going to arrest me for taking what belonged to me." He began to rise from the chair.

Crowley stood up and leaned in toward Kurtz. "Could you give me the names of your business associates so that I can verify your whereabouts for both nights?" The chief could almost see the wheels turning inside Kurtz's head. He did not want to give information about his associates. He was weighing his options.

"Is that really necessary?" Crowley said it was. Joe Kurtz continued, "I'll have to consult my address book which is at my home."

"Please call the station with the names and numbers as soon as possible." Kurtz was rearranging his jacket. The chief added, "And I may need to speak to you again." Crowley looked at the clock. They had been sitting in his office for forty minutes. Crowley thanked Joe for his time.

Joe had his hand on the doorknob when he said, "I had nothing to do with Mr. White's death. I barely knew the man."

Chapter 24

The door closed. Crowley leaned back in his chair, pulled his pipe from his pocket and began filling it with tobacco. Lewis had enough time to complete the task of speaking to Kurtz's wife. The sweet smelling smoke was swirling around his head.

Five minutes later Lewis came in. The patrolman was excited. He had news, but the chief beat him to the punch. "I'm not sure Joe Kurtz is our murderer," Crowley said.

Lewis's mouth opened, "I thought he was your number one suspect," he said.

"Well, he's still a suspect, but he seemed surprised that White was dead. And there was not much of a reaction when he looked at the scissors. Could be he was acting."

The chief shook his head. "He was self-controlled, arrogant, and yet worried. We won't close the door on him." Crowley took a puff on the pipe, and continued, "We'll keep our eyes on him and spread the net wider."

"Maybe Kurtz is just a good actor." Lewis said. His face registered disappointment like a schoolboy who had to stay indoors for recess.

"Mr. Kurtz will be calling the station with names and phone numbers to verify his alibi. We'll check them out and pass the information on to Detective Shiff." There was a lull in the conversation. The chief continued, "I'm sure that the people on that list will say whatever Mr. Kurtz tells them to say. So his alibi is shaky. We'll have to live with that for the time being."

Lewis grimaced. "At least we can give a few names to Detective Shiff."

The chief took a puff, allowing the smoke to swirl past his head. "Now tell me all about your visit with Mrs. Kurtz."

"Yes, that's what I wanted to tell you." Lewis looked concerned. "Mildred Kurtz was like a frightened bird. She was practically twitching when I asked her about her husbands associates. That's when she told me about the man that came to the house on Thursday evening. She said her husband was afraid of him. She heard the name Eddie. He spoke with some kind of an accent, Polish, German, or maybe Russian. She heard bits and pieces of their conversation." Lewis went on to say that Mildred didn't see her husband Monday night, all day Tuesday and Tuesday night. He didn't return until late on Wednesday afternoon."

Lewis unbuttoned his uniform collar. "Storm coming. It's getting humid." It was a rhetorical remark, no answer was needed.

"What did she say he looked like?" The chief asked.

"Big arms, square, stocky, he reminded her of a prizefighter." Lewis stopped and looked at the chief. "She said she didn't get a good look at his face, he kept his hat on and had his back to her most of the time."

The chief placed his pipe in the ashtray. He walked across the room and turned the corkboard to face out. He wrote under the name Joe Kurtz: Alibi? Motive? He then looked over all the cards on the wall and tugged on his mustache, and added another card. This one with the name Eddie on it.

Lewis stood, stretched, lifting his arms and shoulders. "I had a look around, but I didn't see anything that looked suspicious. Of course I didn't go snooping into other rooms or drawers. I didn't want Mildred to get more upset than she already was, poor thing," Lewis said. "I got the feeling she was afraid her husband would come home while I was there. She kept looking out the front window." Lewis shook his head. "I'll be at the front desk if you need anything."

The chief told Lewis to take the rest of the day off. "Go home. There's no money in the budget for overtime." He owed the man his gratitude. "Thanks for all your help."

"Oh that's ok, you know I appreciate the job. Most of my family is in the fishing business and that's a hit or miss paycheck. And right now the fish are moving. The men are trying to figure out what else they can do to make money. Most are turning to lobster for the summer. I like knowing I'll get paid every week." The policeman nodded. "Oh, and there was no shed in the back yard, just a small garden backed by dunes.

Crowley heard the outside door close. The office seemed unusually quiet as he scanned the corkboard. A conversation he had with Harry at his house the other night came to mind. Harry mentioned a man named Eddie, someone at the meeting he'd gone to. Crowley would wait for the undercover cop to make contact.

Crowley took the phone out of its cradle and asked the operator for 1394. The phone was answered by a now familiar voice. The first date had gone well. "Susan, I was hoping you would be free on the last weekend of June," He said.

"How about telling me what you're talking about," Susan had a lilting voice, pleasing to hear.

"Sorry, I'm getting ahead of myself. The fishermen are having a get together. On Friday there's a fish fry and on Saturday there is a dance. It's a fundraiser to bring attention to the fact that the state is considering a bill that will stop access to the waters off the back-beach to night fishing. That would be the Atlantic Ocean to you landlubbers. The fish fry will be held at the Legion Hall and the dance at the Town Hall. I'm hoping you will come with me."

"Sounds like fun. Are you asking me to go to the fish fry or to the dance?" She asked.

"Well, both. I didn't know if you would prefer one or the other, but we could go to both if you like," Crowley said.

"Both would be fun."

Crowley was whistling *Happy Trails* as he headed out of the basement office.

Chapter 25

Crowley woke from his catnap to the sound of the telephone. He was at home in his easy chair with the Standard Times across his lap. He answered saying, "2121." As soon as he heard the voice he knew it was Harry.

"I only have a minute. I'm meeting Joe and a fisherman tonight at the Governor Bradford." Harry spoke rapidly.

Crowley said he understood. "Do you know anything about a guy named Eddie? He works for your new friends, I think."

Harry was in a hurry. "Not someone I'd mess with. Carries a 38 special. We can talk about him later. I gotta go. I'll try to stop by your place late tonight." Harry hung up.

Crowley thought about Eddie. If he carried a gun, why would he stab someone? Why not just shoot him? The chief began answering his own questions. People around? The noise of a gun being fired, the scissors were handy. Or maybe White went after Eddie with the scissors and Eddie got the better of him.

"Scissors can be kept almost anywhere, a bathroom for trimming a beard, in a closet, under a car seat, any room in the house, or in a shed to cut sheet metal." The chief spoke out loud. He didn't want to think about how many scissors were scattered around the homes and offices in town. It was like searching for a needle in a haystack.

Did Mr. White visit Kurtz? Kurtz was lying and his wife was lying for him. That was another possibility. Or maybe the victim got into Kurtz car and was disposed of. Or perhaps he met someone else, went off in another car with his killer? Eddie? Crowley's mind was spinning. He poured himself a whisky and put his feet up on the hassock. Ten minutes later he was asleep.

Late that night Crowley received a visit. A light tap on his back door stirred the chief out of his comfortable living room chair. Harry entered the kitchen. The chief checked his back yard, shut the door, and pulled the shades.

After a brief handshake the older man asked, "Can I get you something to eat or drink?"

"I could use a whiskey." The undercover agent had dark circles under his eyes, he needed a shave, and the chief thought he looked older. Crowley noticed that Harry was wearing a coarse wool jacket liked the Portuguese fishermen wear, even though it was a warm night.

Harry removed the pea coat. "I just came from a meeting at the Governor Bradford. These boys are planning something big. They've hired the fishing boat called *Santina*. Do you know it?"

Crowley poured two fingers of *Old Grand-Dad Kentucky Bourbon* into a glass and handed it to Harry. "I know the boat. A fellow named David Salvador owns it. What's he up to now?"

Harry took a swallow. He made a raspy sound from somewhere deep inside and set the glass down on the kitchen table. "Sounds like you know the fellow."

The chief went to the living room. He picked up his half empty glass and carried it back to the kitchen table. "Our paths have crossed a few times. We had a run-in a couple years back. He was drunk and disorderly. It didn't warrant an arrest." Crowley set his glass down.

He continued, "There was some gossip about him bringing in rum from offshore during prohibition. There was a lot of that at the time. Nothing was proven. That was years ago." Crowley took a sip. "He's known around town to be a hard worker, good fisherman, helpful to his peers." Crowley realized that he liked the fishermen. "I've seen him around town and at the fishermen's association meeting. I understand he's a ladies man."

Harry took a swallow of bourbon. "It sounds like your paths may cross again. I'm supposed to go with him to help out," the undercover cop said. "We'll be meeting a ship off Race Point. I don't have coordinates. There was mention of the last day in June. I'm told it will be a night run. My job is to help load and unload crates. They'll have a truck waiting on the wharf."

Crowley wondered what his department could do to help. "I'm sorry to hear that Captain Salvador is involved." The two men took a moment to think about the gregarious fisherman.

Crowley continued, "That's the night of the fishermen's dance. I'm assuming they are unloading something other than fish. Do you have any idea what is in the crates?" Crowley finished his whiskey in one gulp and set the glass on the table.

"Can I pour you another?" They sat at the kitchen table sipping the second drink. The chief wiped his mustache on a linen napkin from the supply his aunt left in the pantry.

"They don't tell me much," Harry said, "but from what I've overheard it sounds like they're heavy. The captain said he would use his boom and winch to haul the boxes on and off the boat. Salvador needed a third man to help secure them. He'll have one guy with him. I'll be the third."

The Boston cop savored the whiskey then continued, "I spent my summers with fishermen up north. Uncle owns a lobster business. They liked that. Even though I've only been with these fellows for two weeks, they trust me. They think all fishermen are liars or on the wrong side of the law."

They could hear the ticking of the grandfather clock in the living room. "I stay with the crates all the way to Orleans. That should lead us to the men in charge. My boss is pretty excited about the prospects." Harry reached into his jacket, pulled out a pack of Pall Mall. "Do you mind?" he asked, shaking one out of the pack. He didn't light it.

He offered one to Crowley who shook his head no.

"I'm of the opinion the crates contain guns. I won't be able to get away after tonight. I won't be back." Harry paused and smiled, "unless it's for a summer vacation." His eyebrows went up and his sandy hair fell onto his forehead. He looked more like the young man that Crowley had first met. His smile was infectious. "I'll do what I can to help. I can position Lewis on the wharf. He'll watch the boats from the Atlantic Coast Fisheries' office. It overlooks the harbor and the wharf where the *Santina* ties up. Lewis knows the boats. It won't be a problem." Crowley said.

The Chief thought for a few moments then added, "He'll keep out of sight and radio me when the boat leaves the wharf. I'll be waiting somewhere nearby. I'll follow the truck. Always good to have another set of eyes."

Crowley knew that Lewis would love this assignment. He added, "And don't worry about anyone overhearing us. We have our own code, one that just Lewis and I use." The chief laughed out loud, then caught himself and was quiet while he thought.

"I'll be very discrete. Your boss would agree. It's better to have me follow, just in case something goes wrong." The two men sat in silence.

"On another subject, what do you know about this Eddie fellow?" The chief wanted all the information he could get on the man. "Joe Kurtz's wife said she thought Joe was afraid of the man."

Harry recalled his run in with Eddie and shook his head before saying, "His nickname says it all, Eddie The Enforcer."

The temperature in the kitchen was dropping. The chief took another sip from the whiskey as Harry continued. "He drives a Dodge pick up, older model, maybe a 36. I ran into him in Orleans the other night. He was carrying a snub nose 38 special. I got a good look at it when he stuck it in my face."

Crowley told the detective what he knew from the interview with Mrs. Kurtz. "From the description she gave, it sounds like the same man. Mrs. Kurtz said her husband had heated words with him. Joe was alarmed at the man coming to his home. Her husband was frightened." Crowley stopped and thought about the frail woman.

"Eddie is capable of anything," Harry said.

"What about Shiff? Have you called him?" The chief asked.

Harry nodded, "Yes. He wants me to stay undercover. He's swamped in Boston, but he knows where we'll be in Orleans when the crates arrive. He's working something out with his pals at the Bureau. I'm sure they're planning a big surprise for our new party members."

Except for the sound of mice scurrying inside the kitchen wall, it was as quiet. Looking toward the scratching sound, the chief said, "I met some of the FBI guys last winter. It was a big case for them. People were running for their lives, trying to escape Hitler. They had no papers. Most were Jews, fleeing the oppression in France and Germany."

Crowley remembered the maritime operation that led to a freighter carrying people instead of the gold that they were hoping for. "Not exactly what we wanted. In the long run we caught a murderer and helped some people get clear of the war that is swallowing Europe."

The chief was ready with some friendly advice. "This is a dangerous job, Harry. You're dealing with dangerous people. Be extra careful. Someone murdered Frank White and I'm pretty sure it's all connected. Keep your eyes and ears open and be careful what you say." He paused, took a last drink from his glass, and then added, "And you have my sincere thanks for doing this."

Harry brushed his hair back from his forehead. "Just doing my job," he said. "This may uncover a nest of Nazis with big plans. From what I'm hearing these men want to do damage to our government, our country. At the meetings they talk openly about the destruction of our political system. And from what the radio is saying about Herr Hitler, they seem a very violent organization."

There were stories in the newspapers and on the radio daily

about the war on the other side of the Atlantic. After the Great Depression there was a cushion of good years for most Americans. People were working, alcohol was legal again, and music was upbeat. Most citizens didn't understand the brutality that was happening in Europe. They didn't see it. It didn't affect them.

In April of 1934 thousands of people calling themselves The America First Committee held a rally at Madison Square Garden in New York City. They called for the U.S. to stay out of the European conflict, not take sides against Germany. Under pressure, Congress passed the Neutrality Act in 1935. This embargo on trading in arms and war materials allowed the government to be seen as remaining neutral.

Reports of slave camps, destruction, and death were building a great wave of retaliation. America was struggling with becoming involved in the European conflict. Up to this time the United States preferred isolationism.

The President was slow to act. Many Americans supported Great Britain and France, urging President Roosevelt to repeal the Neutrality Act. It wasn't until 1941 that the embargo was finally lifted allowing arms to flow legally to England and France. America sent shipments of fuel, food, and medicines, but the guns and ammo didn't make it until we became involved in the fighting.

There was silence for a few minutes. Both men needed sleep. They finished their drinks and Harry stood up. Crowley picked up both their glasses, placed them in the sink, and then put his hand on Harry's shoulder. "You're doing a great service for your country and I have a feeling you'll be helping me solve a murder as well."

They shook hands. Crowley switched the kitchen light off before opening the back door. He glanced around his yard and listened. "It looks quiet. Take care of yourself." Harry disappeared into the night.

Chapter 26

Lightning and thunder created a sense of excitement as the storm moved across Cape Cod Bay. In the barn a small group of sympathizers had finished their regular meeting. The audience had been sparse this evening. The few members in attendance fled before the soaking spring rain began in earnest. Four men remained, Joe Kurtz, Harry, Eddie, and the man in charge, known to them as Mr. Smith or Smitty. They cleared the room of chairs and stacked them along the back wall. After the salute to Herr Hitler signaling an end of the gathering it had been announced that all meetings for the following month had been cancelled. Only the four men who were stacking chairs knew that the facility was needed for storage.

The barn was quiet. The men stood in a semicircle. "In April I spoke to a couple of fishermen from Provincetown," Joe began, "We joked about who did the most illegal trading in days gone by. Everyone agreed that one fisherman was the best at skirting the law." Joe Kurtz had been told that this guy brought in the most rum during prohibition, made the most money, and owned a fast boat called the *Santina*. "I've met with him three times," Joe told the group.

Mr. Smith stood with his hands in his pockets, looking at Kurtz, waiting to hear the rest. Eddie held his place next to Smith. Harry leaned against the wall close enough to hear what was being said, but not joining the conversation.

"I met the captain at the *Old Colony Tap*." Joe Kurtz continued the story of how he had met the fisherman. "We had a quiet talk at a corner table. Salvador turned out to be just the man we are looking for."

Kurtz remembered their first meeting. The captain was five

feet ten inches, with broad shoulders and arms like bands of iron. His skin was thick, weathered to the color of coffee. His black hair curled around his ears accentuating a wide smile of flawless white teeth. The waitress that brought them beer was openly flirting with the fisherman, rubbing up against him and telling him she would be off at midnight.

Joe bought the beers and asked about fishing. Later they talked about the captain's rum-running days. The fisherman liked to brag about his nights outsmarting, outrunning and outthinking the Coast Guard. "Since the ending of Prohibition there has been no side work for me. So I fish." Salvador had told him. "And fish money barely pays the bills." The conversations had been jovial until Joe began talking about hiring a boat and crew, then things turned serious.

Back at the barn the boss wanted to hear more about the captain. "Will this guy keep his mouth shut and not ask questions? That's what I'm paying for. I don't like the sound of bragging." The boss jingled some coins in his pocket. He looked at Joe Kurtz.

The wind had picked up. The rustling of leaves and a crisp splattering of rain could be heard on the roof. Thunder rolled. Inside the high ceiling barn the men stopped to listen. Joe Kurtz broke the spell. "This captain said he needs the money. He didn't want to know what we were bringing in. He told me that he'd been involved in running rum from Jamaica during prohibition, never caught. He assured me that he had a sea worthy vessel that could outrun the local Coast Guard."

The men in the room waited for the boss to speak, but Joe continued, "I believe he's the kind of guy you can count on, no questions asked. He's being paid well. This is a busy harbor. Vessels come and go at all hours of the day and night. We won't be noticed." Kurtz let this sink in and then added, "Salvador agreed that the best night to make the run is when all the men from the

Race Point Coast Guard Station, most of the fishermen, and many of the townspeople will be at the dance at the town hall."

Joe had asked questions and got the right answers and the information he needed. "Saturday night would be the perfect night. There won't be a moon. It's all set." Kurtz was pleased with his choice of captain and boat. "He'll do what he's told and keep his mouth shut."

The boss smiled, his eyes narrowed, and Harry was reminded of his grandmother's barn cat. Smith patted Joe on the back. "Good. I'll have a truck ready. Joe I want you to talk to this captain again. Tell him I want our supplies back at the town wharf by three AM. Got it?" Kurtz's head bounced in agreement. "I want the truck loaded and on the road before daybreak."

Harry listened to the conversation. He asked, "When do you want me to board the *Santina?*"

The boss gave a slight nod of his head and Joe took over. "I think you should be on the boat early evening. Stay below and keep out of sight." Joe smiled. He liked giving orders. "Captain Salvador will be on board." Kurtz looked at Harry then added, "Just do what the captain tells you."

They could hear the rain whip across the roof sounding as harsh as the boss's voice. Joe Kurtz growled when he continued, "The truck will meet you at Fishermen's Wharf. If he's not there, you wait. Understood?"

Harry shrugged. "I'll wait, that's what you're paying me for. I just hope we don't have to wait all night."

Eddie spoke up for the first time. "What's the matter, afraid you won't get your beauty sleep? Big boy like you should be able to handle one night staying up late." The Enforcer laughed. He pulled a handkerchief out of his pocket and blew his nose. "Don't worry, sonny boy, I'll take care of you."

Harry's answer came quick. "I don't need you taking care of me, I can take care of myself. And how come you're not going on the boat? Get seasick, do you?" He was taunting the big man, goading him, seeing how far he could push.

The upper edge of Eddie's mouth rose on one side, he replied, "I'll be there waiting for you, making sure you do as you're told." His words were soft almost whispered. "You'll come with me in the truck, so I can keep a personal eye on you." Harry could feel goose bumps rise up on his arms. The man radiated violence. You could almost see the sinister streak that ran the length of his body, like the white stripe on the back of a skunk. He enjoyed playing a cat and mouse game with Harry.

To amplify his words, Eddie slid his hand inside his jacket pocket and pulled out a knife. He pressed an unseen button and the blade sprang from the handle. Eddie didn't say anything. He used the tip of the blade to remove what appeared to be grease and dirt from underneath his fingernails. His point was made. Harry didn't blink but didn't ask further questions.

"Why don't the two of you take it outside? Have a smoke." Joe said. It was not a question. He was telling them to take a walk so that he could speak in private to their boss. "And don't let me hear you complain about a little rain." Harry wished he could stay and listen, but he did as he was told.

Joe Kurtz turned to his boss as soon as the two men were gone. "I was asked to stop at the police station yesterday, Chief Crowley wanted to talk to me. I didn't call you because I wanted to see you in person. It's not something we can discuss over the phone." The two men had long ago decided that any important information would be shared face to face at a secure location. If necessary they used a prearranged code word and a meeting would be arranged.

"He took me by surprise, I can tell you. I was unprepared for what he said." Kurtz's had opened his jacket and removed a white handkerchief. His hands were shaking.

The boss's name was Herman Eisling, but years ago he had changed it to Manny Smith in order to sound more American.

No one knew much about the man who they referred to as *Smitty*. He stood a foot taller than Joe, but was much thinner. Wisps of hair lay over his balding head like gray threads over a billiard ball. When he spoke at their meetings he commanded the room with words that were educated and biting. He preached about the oppressed masses and government repression.

"Well, well, the police chief? What did he want?" the boss said. Whether it was concern, fear, or just curiosity the timber of his voice did not change. He was as cool as they come. This man who called himself Manny Smith knew it was not against the law to hold meetings and so far they had managed to keep their gatherings from drawing any publicity or unwanted attention. There was a lot of support outwardly for what they proposed, non-intervention in Europe, meaning they would not fight against Germany. Smith continued, "Did it have anything to do with our meetings?"

"It's worse than that. It's Frank." He let the name hang in the air, not for effect but because he didn't want to be the one bringing bad news. "He's dead."

The boss did not speak for several minutes as if a switch had been turned off. He stood motionless. "Shit." The man in the brown shirt and black tie appeared to be shaken. His face became pink and he rubbed his chin. "This can only mean trouble for us."

Kurtz's neck muscles tightened. "The police chief asked if I knew him. I was seen taking the box of flyers from Frank's car. And he wanted to know where I was last Monday and Tuesday." Kurtz was visibly shaking. He wiped his brow with the handkerchief.

"I understand Frank's car has been impounded. I know you bought that Olds for Frank to use, but it's in the hands of the police now," Kurtz said to his boss.

"Never mind the car, it was in Frank's name, and can't be traced back to me. What did he tell you about Frank?" He was getting impatient.

"Crowley is a sly one. He didn't say much. Just that they were looking into his death. But from the way he questioned me, I'd say it's serious." Kurtz thought about how surprised he was when the chief told him. The old barn they were standing in creaked with the wind. The floor smelled of dried manure. They both looked around the empty space, avoiding the other's eyes.

Joe Kurtz knew that the rest of his story would not go over well with the boss either. "I thought Frank had gone on a bender or run off with some floozy. Crowley wanted to know where I was on Monday and Tuesday nights. I needed an alibi. I had to give him the names of a couple of people who were with me." The boss made a growling noise in his throat. Kurtz had given the names of two party members to the chief of police. The two men stood quietly, each thinking how this would affect them.

The rain on the roof could be heard over their breathing. Kurtz continued, "I was with John Oaks and Pete Shelly. I've already spoken to them. They'll tell the police we were together that night in Hyannis, talking business. They'll vouch for me."

Smith loosened the knot of his tie. "I don't like any involvement with the police. You know that. Our shipment date is set. We need to get the crates and move them quickly. We'll close down the barn and move our operations to Waverly once we have our merchandise."

Smith brought his eyebrows together, his lips tightened, and then he asked, "And what about this new guy, Harry? Eddie told me he was here the other night, alone, coming from the side of the barn. Where'd you get him? He's moved up rather rapidly in our little organization. Do you trust him? Remember it's your neck on the line."

"Yeah, he's ok. Met him in at the *Whydah Tavern* in Orleans. We got to talking. He's just a guy who needed a job. I set up a foolproof trap for him. He passed the test. He didn't open the boxes on any of the deliveries. He's on time and doesn't ask questions. He's not a problem, just a guy down on his luck looking for a payday."

The boss began pacing across the dirt floor. "Frank is another matter," Smith said.

Kurtz shook his head. "You don't suppose Eddie had anything to do with this, do you?" Joe Kurtz asked.

"Fucking Eddie is capable of anything. I've seen him fly off the handle. We need to find out what happened to Frank? We can't let Frank's death get in the way of our plans, not at this late date." He stopped pacing and stood close to Kurtz, only inches from his face. Kurtz could smell the garlic and cabbage on this breath. "He was more than just a deliveryman, he did some things for me, but more important than that, he knew a great deal about our business. Do you think he's been talking to anyone? Maybe he was working both sides of the street, selling information?"

The boss's voice began to rise as if he needed to speak louder due to the rain and wind. "We've got to find out what Frank was up to," Smith said.

"Damn, this is not what I need right now. Things are in motion. I've got a contract. There's money been paid, my money on the line," Smitty's voice became gruff. He tightened his fists. "To be on the safe side, I want you to keep an eye on Eddie and I want Eddie to keep an eye on the new guy. I don't want any more surprises?"

Rain splattered against the side of the building. "I'll speak to those two outside, one at a time," the boss said. "Tell Eddie I want him first. Tell Harry to wait a minute. I'll talk to him after Eddie. Then send them home."

Joe nodded and headed for the side door. Smith stopped him and said, "This deal is very important to me. I don't want you talking to anyone, especially the police. Now is not the time to do or say anything foolish. You're to keep a low profile. Understood?"

As an after thought he added, "Do you think the police are watching you?"

Joe stopped in his tracks. "I don't think so. I've been cautious. Checked carefully, I'm sure I wasn't followed here. I think once the police chief heard from Oaks and Shelly he'd have to believe I had nothing to do with Frank's death. I wasn't in town when he died."

"Alright, send in the boys, one at a time and keep in touch. If you hear anything, call me. If it's important we can meet in Wellfleet at the *Winslow Tavern*."

Joe pulled his hat tight on his head, buttoned up his Macintosh as protection against the weather, and closed the door. After telling the boys to see the boss he headed for his car, relieved that Smith didn't hit the roof when he heard about Frank. Then Kurtz thought about Harry. The boss's questions had raised his awareness about the ease with which the two had met. Could it be nothing, but he did show up just when he was needed, just after Frank disappeared.

Smith questioned Eddie and was satisfied with his answers. Eddie was then instructed to keep an eye on Harry and told in no uncertain terms that there was a great deal to lose. "Make sure this new guy is on the up and up. I don't want any slip ups, understand?"

Harry shook the rain from his hat and held it in his hands. He answered Smith's questions, no hint of guilt or fear in his voice. Harry didn't know Frank White, had never heard of the man, and didn't know anything about his death. Mr. Smith asked about his background, where he had worked before, where he'd lived, and a few questions about his political affiliations. Smith let Harry go after half an hour of questioning.

Chapter 27

Windshield wipers slapped against the glass, barely keeping up with the heavy rain. Harry squinted as he tried clearing the vapor that had collected on the inside of the windscreen. He wanted to stop for a meal and a beer, but more importantly he wanted to be sure he wasn't followed. His usual paranoia, but he knew where to look and could see the signs. The boss's talk with Joe Kurtz alone, without prying ears, he could understand that, but calling them in separately was suspicious as if he were giving Eddie a job that he didn't want Harry to know about. Like following him.

The talk with the boss had gone well, but Harry wasn't taking any chances.

Headlights against the gray cloth ceiling of his Chevy Model Y made Harry a bit jumpy. It didn't mean that it was Eddie. He couldn't get a good look at the vehicle behind him, but the rain was also a good cover for him. Harry decided to stop in Orleans.

Harry slowed his Model Y, allowing the car in back of him to get closer. It was a pick up truck like the one Eddie drove. Harry pulled into the parking lot at the Whydah Tavern, shut off the Chevy's headlights, but kept the engine idling. He took a deep breath and let it out slowly while he watched the taillights of the other vehicle until he could no longer see them.

Without switching on the headlamps, he eased the car out of the parking lot onto County Road determined to get to the peninsula's end and free of prying eyes. He took a right turn onto Old County Road, traveled as far as he dared before relighting the beams. He then he drove roughly three miles.

Harry had scouted out this road on one of his trips to Rhode Island. Early in his career he had learned to keep an eye out for safe places, never knowing when the need would arise. He turned from Old County Road onto a dirt road that was filling in with overgrown brush. It gave Harry a feeling he was entering a tunnel. The road narrowed to ruts that ended at a clearing next to a pond. The rain gave way to foggy mist, giving the night an eerie glow. The combination of moon, fog, and pond gave off a reflection and Harry felt like he was inside a cloud. He shut off the engine and waited for his heart to stop thumping against his chest as if he had run a mile.

Harry pulled out the wool blanket he kept folded on the seat. He pulled up his coat collar, pulled down the brim of his hat, and fell into a fractured sleep. Three hours later the rain had stopped, but a fog still lay over the ground. Harry stirred in the front seat, cracked the window, and lit a cigarette. He needed to see Crowley, let him know the plan. Crowley could pass the news along to Shiff. Tonight would be his only chance to stay clear of Eddie. He was sure the man wouldn't let him get far from his sight again.

Two hours later Harry pulled his car into the lane at the side of Crowley's house. The chief was easily awakened with taps on the glass panel in the kitchen door. He was dressed in the same clothes he'd fallen asleep in and was rubbing his eyes. Harry entered. The chief yawned. The window shades had been pulled down. Crowley lit the small lamp on the wooden table and pulled out a chair for his visitor. They sat. No coffee was offered.

"I've got to be quick, I think I was followed by Eddie tonight, but I lost him in Orleans. Their plan is for Saturday night. Call Shiff for me. Tell him I'm going out on the *Santana*. We're meeting a ship but I don't know the coordinates. A truck will be waiting on Fishermen's Wharf." Harry stopped for a moment then repeated, "Fishermen's Wharf, not Railroad Wharf as I told Shiff a few days ago. Fishermen's Wharf."

Crowley went to the cabinet and took out a bottle of *Old Granddad* along with two glasses. He poured while Harry took off the Portuguese fishermen's hat that he'd taken to wearing. His pea coat gave off the smell of wet wool, musty and sweet.

"I won't be using the phone while I'm in town. There will be no contact from me from now on. Tell Shiff not to worry. They got me a room at the Pilgrim House."

The two men lifted the glasses. "To a safe return," Crowley said. The drinks disappeared.

"Tell Shiff there are at least a dozen crates and they are going to the barn out on Tonset Road in Orleans. He'll know what I mean. I have to go. Let's hope that by Sunday morning we will be having bacon and eggs together at Betty's Luncheonette." Harry quietly left the kitchen and headed back to the center of town.

Two hours later Eddie the Enforcer, having lost Harry in the pouring rain, sat in his Dodge pickup truck parked near the end of Nickerson Street. Eddie needed to talk to Joe Kurtz. He didn't trust the new guy, not after losing him tonight. Kurtz's car was not parked at his home, but Eddie heard Joe brag about stopping to see a woman on his way home. Joe had said he would be back to his wife before morning. Eddie closed his eyes. He was used to waiting for what he wanted.

The rain turned to a fine mist and ghostly damp fog. Eddie could feel it seeping into his clothing. Just after midnight a Ford pick-up truck stopped in front of the Kurtz house and a man in fishermen boots got out. A tap on the front door brought Mildred Kurtz from the interior. They spoke for a few minutes before the stranger put his arms around Mrs. Kurtz and pulled her into a passionate embrace. They kissed, long and hard. Then the man turned away while Joe's wife slowly closed the door. Eddie the Enforcer whistled a small sound and watched the truck pull away.

When dawn was breaking in the eastern sky a '35 Chevrolet Standard Six pulled up at the house. Joe Kurtz got out and went inside. Eddie waited a few minutes then headed to the house. A short sharp knock on the door brought Joe Kurtz to the threshold.

Kurtz didn't look happy. "You'd better come in," Kurtz said. After the door was closed he continued, "What brings you to my house at this ungodly hour?"

"I lost Harry last night. Could have been on purpose, but what with all the rain I couldn't keep him in sight. I thought he'd stopped at the Whydah Tavern but when I got there he was nowhere in sight." Eddie took off his hat and shook the excess raindrops out onto the floor. "I need to know where he's staying. Then I take care of him."

Joe Kurtz frowned at the hulk standing in front of him. "It's not your decision to make. You'll stick to the plan. He's staying at the Pilgrim House, downtown. There's a parking lot out back. He keeps his Ford Model Y there. Easy to spot since there are only a few of that model left around. You know what it looks like. Right?" Joe didn't mind rubbing the man's nose in the dirt.

"This time, don't lose him. The boss wants him watched until after we unload. Understand?" Joe said. Kurtz didn't like this thug coming to his house, he didn't like the man, and he was beginning not to like the business they were running. Kurtz was a Nazi not a smuggler, but the money was good and it would further the cause.

"If there's nothing else, I suggest you head over to the hotel." Joe Kurtz wanted this man out of his house. He walked toward the door.

Eddied put his hat back on, looked at Joe and said, "Can you step outside for a moment."

Joe hesitated as a sharp dagger of fear ran through him. "What do you want?"

Eddied smirked. "Just a quiet word, for your benefit. No need to worry, I'm not going to hurt you." He laughed. Eddie knew the power he held over weak individuals like Joe Kurtz.

The two men stepped out of the house. Eddie square as a slice of bread, Joe looking more like a pear, they walked toward the street. The rain had stopped, the fog lingered, and daylight had arrived. The powerful man said in a whispered voice, "I think you need to keep a better eye on that pretty little wife of yours."

Kurtz's face turned beet-red. He stuttered, "What, what did you say? What are you implying? What's that supposed to mean? Keep your filthy thoughts away from my wife." Joe's voice echoed in the calm damp morning air.

"I'm just giving you a piece of advice. I saw your wife kissing a man on the doorstep of this very house only a few hours ago. I thought you'd want to know." A bark of laughter came from the enforcer. He opened the door of his truck and left Joe Kurtz standing in the foggy mist. Kurtz returned to his house and Eddie headed to the Pilgrim House to pick up where he'd left off.

Eddie was feeling smug. He found a weak spot in Joe's suit and enjoyed making him squirm. Eddie knew all about cheating women, his own wife being one of them. She'd run off with their two children over three years ago and he'd not heard a word from her since.

Eddie grumbled about losing the new man last night. He squirmed in the driver's seat, feeling the heat rise to his temples. He would take care of Harry. He'd cross that bridge when he came to it, when the time was right. The Dodge pickup pulled into the lot at the Pilgrim House and there was Harry's Ford Model Y. Eddie parked next to it.

At noon Harry came out the front door of the hotel, but didn't take his car. He walked right past Eddie. The Enforcer watched Harry all afternoon. He stayed at the hotel in the room next to Harry's. Eddie passed a ten-dollar bill to the clerk at the Pilgrim House asking if Harry used the phone. He had not, but the clerk would let him know if he did.

A phone call from Joe Kurtz on Friday brought Harry to the Governor Bradford at eight o'clock in the evening. The restaurant was busy with locals and tourists. Harry was introduced to Captain Salvador who looked more like a fisherman than anyone

Harry had ever met. Strong arms, black curly hair, boots and a winning smile. A few minutes later Eddie the Enforcer stepped into the bar and joined the small group. Kurtz avoided eye contact with Eddie, acted like he wasn't there, and spoke directly to Harry and the fisherman. The plan was tightened, they discussed their part, and money was exchanged. Once they had finished the business end of the meeting, Eddie ordered the Friday night special. Joe Kurtz excused himself and left. The fishermen said he had to check his boat, leaving Harry and Eddie glaring at each other. Eddie ate with gusto while Harry poked at the meat loaf supper and sipped a whiskey.

"I've checked into the Pilgrim House for the night," Eddie said. "I got a room on the same floor as you." Eddie watched for a reaction, but Harry didn't even blink. He figured that someone would be watching him, so he made no strange moves, and had been above reproach. Eddie continued, "I figured there was no sense driving back and forth, so I stay and get a little rest. I'll pick up the truck tomorrow, and then it's just you and me. We'll go for a little drive together."

If Harry was rattled he didn't show it. He said, "Yeah, just the two of us. Cozy." Inwardly Harry hoped he would be slapping the cuffs on this overgrown Neanderthal at the end of the sting. He looked forward to taking the smirk off his face.

Chapter 28

The clock said three AM. Crowley's mind was swirling, seeing pictures, people, scenes that may or may not exist. He got up earlier than usual and walked the few blocks from his home to the basement office. He was walking because the squad car was parked on Bradford Street, behind the Town Hall.

On the previous afternoon before leaving the office Crowley discussed the plans with Lewis. "We'll leave the squad car on the street for all to see. It will appear we are staying close to the office. Understand? I'm going to be using a different one for Saturday night and we can both walk to work in the morning."

The new day had not yet arrived, the night was not quite over, but both were about to change. Some called this time of day nautical twilight. Captain William O'Donnell was heading for his fishing boat when he met Chief Crowley at the corner of Court and Commercial Streets at daybreak. The fisherman was dressed in knee-high black boots, carried his oil jacket over his shoulder, and held a muslin bag in his hand. The man was known as the best fish storyteller in Provincetown.

"You're up early chief," O'Donnell said. The two men didn't stop, didn't even slow their step, or say good morning, but continued walking side by side. "Can't sleep?" asked the fisherman.

"Something like that," the chief said. "How's fishing?" Even with all the intrigue hanging over the chief's life, he was a romantic at heart. He liked to hear the stories told by the fishermen, especially Captain O'Donnell. The chief recalled many an afternoon sitting next to wood stoves in various shacks, on various piers, and at the Diogo's kitchen table, sucking on his pipe, listening to their tales. Their stories were full of life and death, vividly recalled. They sometimes passed a bottle, sometimes offered coffee and sometime there was nothing but twine in their hands, but they always talked. And so Chief Crowley enjoyed the short walk down Commercial Street with Captain O'Donnell as daylight seeped into the sky.

"Did I ever tell you about the haul I had last summer. Biggest catch in one day I've ever had. The net came back tow after tow with thousands of pounds. The last tow was so big I couldn't get the net back into the boat, must have been over ten thousand pounds of Flounder in there." The fisherman took a breath and looked around, at the still sleeping town. "Yeah, but no one will believe me, they think I made it up. One of the guys said I couldn't fit that much fish in the net at one time, net's too small, but I know for a fact, I was there. I had to rip open the net and let them all swim away."

He shook his head, his mouth forming a grimace as if his teeth hurt. "I only brought in three thousand that day, but I know for a fact that there was ten thousand pounds that I had to let go. There was more fish in that one tow than all of the boats combined landed for the whole day." The fisherman went on about that day, how his boat was the best in the fleet, and how the seas were building that day to the size of mountains. "That boat of mine has a keel that smells fish. She's a lucky boat and carries herself well, even in a foaming swell."

For Chief Crowley, this man was a breath of fresh air. The other fishermen in the fleet had given him the nickname *Major Hoople*, based on the newspaper cartoon character in *Board and Room* by Ken Pierce. William O'Donnell owned and fished the *Wallace and Roy* a Provincetown deep-hulled dragger. It was painted a dark green with an orange mast, the colors that the Provincetown fleet was known to use on their fishing vessels. Rumor had it that the boatyard bought a truckload of dark green paint, on the cheap, and every boat that hauled out was painted the same color.

It wasn't long before William spoke again, "Anything new on the man you found on the beach last week? I know I shouldn't pry but I read about it in the paper. It's the talk of the town right now, that and the fish fry tonight. You're coming?"

"Yes, I'm coming, bringing a friend. But as for the other, well I'm not at liberty to give out any information right now." He paused. "But things are progressing." The chief didn't want further gossip spreading through town so he added, "The man wasn't from here, lived in Gloucester. I should know more in a few days." That seemed to satisfy his companion.

They parted company in front of the Town Hall, each man heading to his place of work. "Have a safe trip," the chief called to the fisherman. O'Donnell nodded, tipped his hat, and headed for the wharf.

Crowley's first call that morning went to Shiff to let him know what was in the works. He told Shiff about Harry. "I've got things covered on this end. I'm looking forward to a pleasant outcome for the *Fishermen's Dance*." It was the code name they had given the operation. This was a case of murder and espionage, Nazis and fishermen. Local, state and federal officers were being pulled together like the pucker strings on the cod end of a fishermen's net.

Crowley opened the door leading to his water closet, took the keys from his pocket, and unlocked the metal cabinet. He checked to be sure his gun was clean and that he had spare bullets. He had cleaned, oiled and fired the gun last week. Taking a deep breath, he relocked the metal safe.

Late Friday morning Crowley and Lewis met in the chief's office to go over their plans for Saturday night. "I'll be using one of Joe Duarte's cars for this raid. It runs good and has new tires. I'm all set." The chief told Lewis to use the radio in the fish buyer's office to signal him. "Use the code we worked out and stay on Channel 16," he said.

Sixteen is the frequency monitored by law enforcement.

It was used by the military, Coast Guard, and by local police departments. "I want to know when the boat leaves and when it returns. Your place in the upstairs office is essential. Keep a tight watch and above all, don't be seen, no lights. I believe they will unload the cargo quickly and leave the area hoping no one will notice. We don't know the exact timing, so stay alert."

Lewis was told not to arrest Captain Salvador. "He'll go home. He doesn't know we're on to him." At least that's what Crowley hoped for. "And we will want to have a word with his crewman as well, but first things first. It's going to be a long night for the Provincetown Police. Get some sleep tonight." the chief said.

Lewis was eager and unfazed by late night duty. The man could sleep anywhere, but could stay awake when called upon no matter the time. "Salvador has a family and a boat to think of. No, he won't run. And his crewman has a wife and three small kids. He's not going anywhere. Now all we have to do is wait," Lewis said. They would get through today and then tomorrow would come at them full throttle.

After Lewis left the office, Crowley called Susan to arrange a time to meet for the fish fry. He had been looking forward to seeing her again.

The next call went to Dr. Rice to let him know that the murder weapon was indeed a pair of scissors like the one brought by the doctor. "Nice to know I am right some of the time," the doc said. "Are you going to the Legion Hall tonight?" When Crowley said he was bringing Susan, the physician said, "I'll save two seats."

Last week Manuel Macara captain of the *Victory* came to the station and sold the chief two tickets to the fish fry. Manuel Macara, not to be confused with Joseph Macara who captained the *Annabella R*, or Norbert Macara who they called Daddy's Boy, had sold Lewis two tickets to the fish fry. He then sold four to Mrs. Gracie who was in the office to complain about a neighbor. She told them that someone was shooting a gun off near her home. "He's shooting in the pitch dark, in the middle of the night, waking us up. I told my husband Leo that I'd see you, but I didn't expect to be buying tickets," she said. "I'm going to give these tickets to my two sons. They can take their wives." The chief wrote himself a note to go to the farm and look into the matter. Mrs. Gracie was reassured.

The chief arrived for Susan at five-thirty and they drove to the Legion Hall, chatting along the way about the weather. A crowded room greeted the couple. A goldfish bowl sat on the glass topped counter next to the entrance. It was full of dollar bills and had "The Fishermen's Fund" printed on a paper taped across the front. The chief added to the fund.

Crowley took Susan's elbow in his large hand and steered her, as if they were dancing, to the end of the line that snaked around the outside walls of the hall. The Police Chief found himself introducing Susan to a number of townspeople, William Cabral the Postmaster, Chester Peck who owned the Provincetown Inn, B. H. Dyer who owned one of the local hardware stores, and a number of fishermen. Everyone smiled and spoke about fish, boats, and weather.

The place felt warm, but not hot because of the southwest wind that blew the heat across the room and out the open windows on the opposite side, leaving behind a sweet smell of rose hip and seawater mingled with the scent of fried fish and steamed lobster. Fried Codfish, cooked lobster in homemade mayonnaise sauce, stuffed sea clams, and hot Portuguese sausage greeted the couple as they offered up their plates.

Laughter from a group in the corner caused Crowley to take his eyes away from the food and Susan. He saw Billy Adams. Billy's expression changed rapidly when he saw the chief looking at him. Crowley imagined a raccoon caught in the headlamps, bewildered and pissed off.

Crowley wondered briefly about Billy and his activities with

Mildred. The chief pushed all thoughts of Billy Adams, Mildred and Joe Kurtz out of his head. There were other things on his mind this night. He was wondering if he should hold Susan's hand. His eyes scanned the room. Good to his word, Dr. Rice waved an arm and pointed to the two empty chairs. The chief and Susan made their way passed men in short sleeves, wearing white aprons, spooning up the food. They carried their trays to the long table where Dr. Rice and his wife were waiting.

Small talk, good food, and a glass of beer made for a successful evening. Crowley asked Doc Rice about the new Oliver baby and was reassured that all was well. Crowley and Susan made their way outside with coffee cups in hand, pausing to watch the water and the sky, pastel colors from the retreating sun reflecting off the bay. The summer Equinox brought high tides and long days. "I'd never heard of a fish fry before and this has got to be one of the best meals I've ever eaten. Thank you for inviting me," Susan said. "I'm looking forward to the dance tomorrow night." She caught the look of surprise on the chief's face.

"Oh, I'm sorry I forgot to tell you, I can't make it. I'm really sorry. I was looking forward to it as well, but I really won't be able to go." Her dinner partner looked sheepish like the young boy he had once been.

Crowley continued, "I've been meaning to tell you. It's part of the job. I have to work." He was rattling on and he knew it.

Susan looked bewildered. "Oh! I was looking forward to it. But I understand. What will you be doing, guarding the dancers?" She was being sarcastic and he knew it.

"No, I'm afraid my business is elsewhere tomorrow night. I'm sorry I can't tell you more, and I'm really sorry I can't go to the dance." They sat together on the porch of the Legion Hall watching the sun disappear below the horizon. There was a sudden chill in the air. "Come on, I'll drive you home," James Crowley said.

Chapter 29

No sun peeked from behind the gray clouds on Saturday morning. Over the next few hours the wind picked up from the east while the sky collected bigger and darker clouds. Harry stepped aboard the *Santina* in the late afternoon, glad to be out of the wind. He rapped on the side of the doghouse, then called below, "It's Harry." He was told to come down.

Harry looked around the small cabin. The ceiling was black with soot from a coal stove that kept the area dry and warm. It made the space dark and dingy, yet at the same time warm and inviting. A kerosene lamp hung from a hook over the table, casting a dull light. The foc'sle smelled of coffee. Bunks on both sides of the forward area were empty. Captain Salvador was sitting at the galley table with a mug between his hands. There was no smile, no greeting.

"I'll give you a tour once you've had some coffee." Salvador got up and took a cup from a hook, pouring the dark liquid. "There's sugar but no milk." His voice was harsh, raspy from too many cigarettes. Harry said he took his black.

A few minutes later the two men were on deck. The captain showed the temporary help around the boat. "I'll operate the winch. You and my crewman will move the boxes to the fish hold as quickly as possible. He won't come aboard until after dark, no reason to. You, on the other hand, are another matter. If anyone asks who you are, I'll say I'm showing the ropes to a new crewman. There will be no mention of this trip out tonight, not to anyone, understand?"

Harry nodded his head in agreement without saying anything. The captain continued showing him around. The fisherman lifted a heavy wooden lid from the center of the deck. "This here's the fish hold. The boxes need to go in there. You will be in the hold. Ernie, my crewman will guide the boxes as I lower them using the block and tackle and a winch. I don't want anything left on deck. Especially if this wind keeps up." He closed the hatch and walked to the small wheelhouse located at the stern of the boat. Harry followed him and the conversation continued while the two men stared out the windows of the fishing vessel.

"How familiar are you with boats? I don't need anyone green and heaving over the side," Salvador said.

It was Harry's turn to speak. "I've spent a lot of time on the water, summers with my uncle up in Maine since I was ten years old. He's out of Portland. I know how to tie a Clove Hitch and a Bowline. I can handle the lines and I don't get sick. You won't have to worry about me," the undercover cop said.

The captain looked the new crewman over. "Right then, let's get you below deck. You might as well crawl into a bunk. It's going to be a few hours. Take the one on the starboard side. Ernie uses the port and I don't think he'd be pleased to see you in it. You'll get supper before we leave. I'll wake you." Harry went into the foc'sle and did as he was told, falling into a fretful sleep.

A rustling of pots and pans woke Harry. It was still light out, although from his position in the bunk the only illumination was a dim glow that filtered in through a slotted door in the doghouse. The world looked gray. "I'm frying up some fish and potatoes, there's enough for you if you want some." The captain remarked.

Harry rubbed the sleep from his eyes and jumped out of the bunk. "I'm starved," he said. "What time is it?"

"We've got plenty of time, it's only nine o'clock. I don't expect to see Ernie until eleven. And we won't be leaving the dock until after he arrives. The dance should be in full swing by then, so we can slip away without notice, and be back before the cock crows." The smell of frying fish made Harry's mouth water.

"Sounds good to me. And it sure smells good in here. What kind of fish are you cooking?" The crewman asked.

"Yellow tail flounder, my favorite. Caught it yesterday." They talked about the weather, fishing, and boats. No mention was made of the job that lay ahead of them. The atmosphere in the cabin was almost jovial.

Harry thought it felt unnatural, as if he was going on a fishing trip. Salvador told fishing stories and talked about his days running rum. "One time we met a sailboat coming up from Jamaica. We fished until we spotted her, then hauled in the net and filled the hold with cases of rum from the island. We covered the shipment with the fish. It was easy getting the bottles aboard, the risky part was unloading. But with fish to cover the merchandise no one was the wiser. Those were the days."

He was a man who liked to hear himself talk, either that, or his chosen field of work, being alone most of his days, gave him a need to communicate. "If one of the wooden boxes was to break and fall we'd have been in deep shit. But the boys never dropped a box." Like so many of the fishermen that Harry met, Salvador showed no fear, seemed to rely on instinct, and used common sense.

There were hard times for many of the fishermen and this captain was no different. He had problems. "I'm in hock up to my eyeballs. And there's not enough fish in the ocean to pay all the bills. I had to put in a new engine last year when the old one blew up." Then he changed tack and began telling more stories of outrunning the law, sailing from Morocco to Florida on a Danish built yacht. The captain apparently loved the sea and his freedom. Harry wondered about the man, part fisherman, part pirate, and part something else.

Harry stretched out on the bunk and listened. The cabin smelled of fried fish. Water sloshed between the wharf's pilings, and the side of the hull, in a haphazard rhythm, a sure sign that the wind was breezing up. Harry was aware that the captain seemed without regard to the wind, choppy water, or darkening sky. Before Salvador retreated to the wheelhouse he told Harry to stay below when they cast off. "My crewman and I will handle the lines. We're used to our jobs and I don't want you getting in the way."

Harry didn't say anything and the captain continued in a loud gruff way, "When we're underway and clear of the harbor you can wander around. Come to the wheelhouse, or stay on deck, or stay below, whatever you decide. Just stay inside the boat," the captain laughed as he gave his new man orders.

At eleven o'clock another man climbed aboard and went directly into the cabin. He tipped his hat to the captain. Salvador then went into the engine room and the next thing Harry heard was the roar of a diesel engine. The lines were quickly cast off and the boat made its way out to sea, passing Long Point Light on their starboard side. The seas were short, choppy inside the cove. The boat passed the tip of land, bringing it into open water.

The sea on this night was rolling in from the north and east, a rolling-swell cresting at the top, bringing foam to the curl. The boat moved with yawl and sway like a grandmother rocking a child, as it slid along the sea. The Detroit engine hummed inside the hull while the boat moved steadily forward. The wind gave them a gentle push as the *Santina* made her way farther from land.

During the journey Harry vacillated between the sheer amazement of being out on the ocean at night and the terror of wondering what this unusual night might bring. Harry was sure-footed, quick and knew he could handle the lines. He'd been hauling and moving lobster cages since he was a kid. Harry knew about block and tackle, he understood the mechanics of winches, and the physics behind lifting heavy loads. He was comfortable on a moving deck. His uncle, a fisherman, told him he was a natural on the water and taught him well.

Schooling was a priority in the house where Harry grew up.

Instead of finding a career on the water he spent four years at the University of Massachusetts. He thought he would study law, but instead opted for the Police Academy. He then began a career with the BPD. The job ahead was what he'd been training for and what waited on land was a part of the job.

Chapter 30

A few miles north of Race Point, the wind was picking up and all daydreams became focused on what lay ahead of them. All three men on the *Santina* saw the freighter at the same time. Approaching the vessel was like coming up to a canyon wall, dark, flat and solid. When they were close enough to read the name on the bow, the *Maura Marie,* the three men raised their chins toward the sky in order to see the deck of the ship.

The sea rolled in from offshore. Salvador chose the lee side of the ship and the crew made ready for the exchange. The fishermen put old tires out over the side to act as fenders. Lines were unfurled from the deck of the freighter, tied to cleats on the fishing boat, and then a rope ladder was lowered from the offshore vessel. From the deck of the freighter, the arm of a crane was moved out and away, over the top of the fishing boat. It would be used to lower the boxes from the mother ship. The smaller boat bounced in the chop but the larger vessel did not move, as if she were standing her ground. Salvador quickly climbed the ladder, disappeared for ten minutes, then returned and climbed back aboard the *Santina.* "We're ready," the fisherman said.

"Harry, get into the fish hold. Arrange the crates as I told you, inside the fish-pens, one to starboard, next to port, on either side of the keel walk. Three pens on a side, stack the boxes two per pen, and don't forget to put the pen boards in. From the top down, the boards will slip in along the groves to keep those suckers from moving around. Got it?" Harry nodded his head. He understood.

Salvador turned back, "One more thing." He looked directly into Harry's eyes. "If anything goes wrong," the fisherman paused, "you're on your own." The captain waved his arm and the boxes, looking like small coffins, were lowered, one at a time. Salvador and his crewman maneuvered the crates carefully to the opening of the fish hold. It took all three men to lower each into the hull.

Harry discovered how heavy the boxes were when he let the first one land in the center of the hull and not in the pen. He had to push, twist, pull, and slide the wooden box until it was safely placed in the first fish-pen. He hollered to the men on deck to give more slack to the rope. The second box went easier. He used the ropes to swing the heavy object into place on the opposite side as he'd been instructed, before he let it settle in place. The box landed with a thud, but with less effort.

As his task proceeded he was able to move the boxes with more precision. As soon as a crate was in place, the line was whipped back to the freighter to begin the task again. Harry was nimble. He kept his feet away from the heavy boxes as he swung them into the pen and let the line go.

A rhythm was established and the work went smoothly. After forty minutes the fish hold held all it's illegal catch. The pen-boards were in place and twelve crates were secured. Harry was anxious to get out from below deck. He watched from the opening of the doghouse as the ladder was swiftly removed, the lines untied, and the fenders brought aboard, allowing the *Santina* to pull away from the side of the steel ship. The fishing boat was considerably lower in the water as they headed back to town.

The vessel was in her element. Seawater splashed over the bow as the vessel plowed into the waves. An occasional jarring movement brought the reality that he was in an old boat, carrying a cargo of explosives through a building sea with two guys he didn't know. He worried about a crate becoming loose. It could pierce the hull sending them all to Davy Jones in a matter of minutes. When Harry asked the crewman about that, Ernie chuckled and told Harry not to worry. "We've hauled cargo before. This little boat can hold tens of thousands of pounds. You go tell the captain everything is ship shape, neatly stowed."

Harry made his way across the moving deck as showers of spray pelted him before he stepped into the wheelhouse. "Getting rough, but this is a tight little ship you've got here. She's seaworthy that's for sure."

"That she is," he answered. "This is a vessel that likes to have her belly full. Usually with fish." The captain looked at Harry and asked, "What brings you into the wheelhouse?"

"Your crewman said to tell you everything in the fish hold is secure." Harry watched the captain light a cigarette.

"You did a good job with the crates," Salvador said. "Now all we have to do is get them off without a fuss." He took a puff and blew the smoke toward the ceiling. "I'll use the mast, a double block and tackle to get them into the truck. Just like we did earlier, only in reverse. This time, my man Ernie will be in the hold. He'll tie up the crates. I'll run the wench and you will guide them up and into the truck. Got it?"

Harry said he understood. The captain went on, "A tag line is attached to the cargo. You'll use that to maneuver them. There will be a couple of guys in the truck. We need to get them off as quickly as possible. This is the most dangerous part. Once we start there's no turning back."

"I got it. I can handle my end. Will one truck handle this load?" Harry asked. They spoke as cohorts, as men of the sea, but not as friends. Harry was hoping they would have only one vehicle to follow.

"Your boss said he would use a one-ton truck," the fisherman said. "If there's a problem he'll send two of his smaller delivery trucks. One truck would be quicker for us. Either way, these babies get delivered tonight. I'm risking a lot. I want them gone, I want my money, and I want you off my boat. No hard feelings, but I don't want to see you again." He looked out the wheelhouse window. "This is the last time I work for these guys, I don't need the aggravation, and my stomach can't handle any more of this.

Your friends are the worst of the worst." The fisherman knew how precarious his situation was.

Harry stepped out of the wheelhouse and lit a cigarette. The captain was not only taking a chance of being caught, he didn't seem to know what was being delivered. He was trusting people who were basically untrustworthy, people who didn't give a rat's ass about Salvador or his boat. If Salvador knew what was in the boxes, he hadn't asked. It was all about the money. Harry picked up his head, tossed the cigarette into the sea, and stared into the pitch-black night. He felt like he was suspended between earth and sky, heaven and hell, no up or down, no time or space, just inky dark on a rolling deck.

The wind was steady from the east, not yet a gale, but definitely threatening. The little vessel made the trip back to port in just over two hours. Rounding the tip of Cape Cod at Long Point, the wind eased as they came closer to land. The captain could just make out a dot of light on the top of a pole, at the end of the pier. He headed for the light. Another fifteen minutes and they were placing lines on the poles.

Salvador climbed the ladder and looked around. There was only one truck parked on the pier. The fisherman struck a match and the vehicle began to move, backing up. The cargo door, made of canvas, was rolled up. The truck moved closer to the *Santina's* rail.

Eddie the Enforcer jumped down from the passenger side of the truck. Another man in a long coat and peaked cap stepped from the driver's side. Harry didn't recognize the second man who then leaped onto the cargo space of the truck. The vehicle reminded Harry of the trucks used for wholesale products that were appearing more and more around the state. It was big enough to carry this heavy load with room to spare.

The men got straight to work. There was no discussion. Everyone seemed familiar with the procedure. Harry worked the tag line without difficulty as the crates were hoisted from the fishing boat to the back of the waiting vehicle. The tide was high, giving them ample room to maneuver the boxes as they were hoisted from the fish hold. The sound of the wind could be heard whistling in the rigging above the rumble of the truck's engine. Unloading went fast. Pickup and delivery had taken five hours. Harry looked at his wristwatch. It was ten past three o'clock in the morning. They were right on schedule.

The undercover cop watched Eddie take an envelope from the inside pocket of his coat and hand it to Salvador. They did not shake hands. The fisherman went back to his boat without saying a word to Harry. Harry could almost see the relief on Salvador's face. A twinge of regret passed through Harry as he thought about the captain sitting in Chief Crowley's jail. There was something redeemable, even likeable about this adventurous fisherman.

Harry was sweating under the woolen jacket. The temperature felt as if it had risen ten degrees since he had come ashore. There was no removing his outer coat because of the holster he wore under his left armpit.

"Well, that went smoothly." Eddie the Enforcer grinned at Harry. "Nice to see you again, Harry. How was your trip?" Harry muttered something about easy going. The driver climbed in behind the wheel. Harry sat in the middle with Eddie on his right, on the outside. As they drove away from the wharf, not one of the three men glanced at the building where boats were tied on three sides, where seafood was unloaded, and where a second floor office looked down on the wharf.

Lewis had been standing or sitting in the shadows of the second floor building belonging to Mr. Cabral, a local fish-buyer, since just after dark. The policeman had a bird's eye view of the harbor, the wharf, and the boats. He watched the fishing boat leave, heading toward Long Point with one crewman on deck.

There were no running lights in the rigging. The boat moved away from the wharf and disappeared from sight within minutes.

As the *Santina* pulled away, Lewis picked up the microphone, and pressed the key on the side. "The dance is in full swing. Look's like it's going to be a hopping night. No complaints from the town hall." he said. There was no reply.

Lewis sat with his chair pushed away from the window, looking out across the wharf and harbor. It was a dark night, no stars, just grey on black, with streaks of white caps across the water. The fishing fleet was tied on moorings, bows pointing up into the wind, tugging at their lines. The fishermen had a saying *East is Least, West is Best.* It was practical to remain tied up when a storm was brewing. The wind and the Fishermen's Dance kept the boats in the harbor on this night. On a usual morning at three o'clock, some boats were already heading to the fishing grounds. There was only one boat moving this night and if a person hadn't been watching closely, they would have missed it. The boat was a black spot on the horizon, hardly visible.

Lewis watched gray water and gray sky when the silhouette disappeared from view. Positively identifying a boat by its silhouette was something that the Provincetown policeman was proud of. And he was very good at it. As the *Santina* came closer, returning to the wharf, Lewis was on the radio again. "The dance is over. I'm heading home," he said. "All is quiet in town."

The response came quickly. "Roger that," was all that the chief said. Crowley was waiting in a Chevy Coupe, parked just a few yards from the corner of Bradford and Commercial Streets. Using the Provincetown Police Department's squad car was impossible because it was easily recognized. The painted decals on the sides, the rather large spotlight above the mirror, and the red light mounted on the front roof would give him away. He had to follow the gangsters to their destination without being noticed, not easily done in the middle of the night when traffic was negligible.

Crowley's borrowed vehicle had good visibility and was fast. When the chief saw the one-ton truck cross the road in front of him, he counted to sixty and slowly followed, leaving plenty of distance between them. Crowley hoped they were heading for Tonset Road. But just in case the plan changed, or something went wrong, the chief could not loose sight of the truck, not with his friend Harry sitting in the front seat. He stayed well back.

Near Blackfish Creek in Wellfleet the chief picked out two red dots in the distance looking like tiny ruby eyes that seemed to be leading him to the dragon's lair. They made their way along County Road. A few vehicles passed him during the forty-minute ride, grocery, milk and newspapers deliveries, or an early morning fisherman on his way to the beach.

Crowley had taken his service weapon from the lock-box in the office closet before he left the station. He patted the holster under his left arm as if to be sure it was still there. The chief felt the weight of it, making him uncomfortable. He hadn't fired the gun in weeks. James had learned how to care for weapons while serving in the Army and again at the Police Academy. He didn't like the idea of having it strapped to his body or having to use it. It was there only for protection.

Chapter 31

Saturday evening before the Fishermen's dance began, before the *Santina* set sail, and before any plans were put into action, Mr. and Mrs. Kurtz were having a loud and heated argument inside their home on Nickerson Street. "You are going with me and that's final," shouted Joe Kurtz.

"No. I don't want to go to Orleans." Mildred was surprised by her own voice and the ferocity with which she spoke. "Why all of a sudden do I have to go with you? I don't want to go to one of your meetings." She had never before stood up to the man she had married. "I'm staying here," her voice quivered as she stood her ground.

Suddenly, Joe Kurtz exploded and slapped her across her face. Then hit her a second time with the back of his hand. "You will do as you are told," he screamed.

She fell across the bed and lay whimpering. Fire burned on her bruised cheek. Her heart felt like stone.

Joe raised his hand to strike again. "There's more where that came from. I'm not in the mood for any of this. Get an overnight bag packed. Now!"

Mildred didn't move. She stared at him, shocked. She could read the hatred in his eyes and was terrified beyond anything she could understand. She felt powerless. Without saying another word, she stood. She straightened her dress and pulled a bag from the closet. After she put on her shoes, she put a change of clothing a few toiletries into the case. When she was done she picked it up and followed her husband out of the bedroom.

"You will stay in the big house with Mrs. Smith while I go to the meeting in the barn. Do you understand? You will no longer remain at home when I go out on business. I've made arrangements for you. You'll stay with Mrs. Smith for the night. She's agreed, has plenty of room, and you can help her make breakfast for the men." His voice was icy, yet calm as if they were planning a holiday. "There will be no discussion," he said. She caught a glimpse of the sneer on his face.

Mildred knew he couldn't see what was in her heart, couldn't read her thoughts, but somehow her husband knew. He had discovered her relationship with Billy. It was the only explanation. Maybe Crowley said something, although he promised he wouldn't. Maybe a neighbor had seen Billy and told Joe. However it had occurred, she knew that everything was about to change and she felt an overwhelming sorrow as if her life were ending. Mildred did as she was told. She followed her husband out to the car.

At the same time, love struck, hoping for a glimpse of Millie, Billy took the short drive up Nickerson Street. He needed time to think, to put together the puzzle that was his life. After parking the truck, he watched the house as an amazing scene unfolded in front of him. His heart began to pound and his breath came in short gasps.

Millie came out of the house carrying a small suitcase. Her head bowed. She didn't look up. Her thin wool coat hung to her ankles, appearing to be two sizes too big for her as if she had suddenly shrunk. Joe Kurtz locked the front door behind him, pulled the fedora hat down to his brow, and went around to the driver's side without helping his wife.

Joe Kurtz hesitated briefly. He scanned his surroundings before he got into the Chevy and drove off. Billy ducked. Kurtz didn't turn his head, didn't look at either side of the street, just stared straight ahead. At the corner of Nickerson and Bradford, Kurtz's car turned left. Billy followed.

It was Saturday night, tourist season was beginning, and the fishermen were holding a dance at the Town Hall. The road was busy. Inside the '35 Chevrolet the Kurtz's were silent. Joe had a white-knuckles grip on the steering wheel. Mildred sat as close to the passenger door as she could get, staring out the window, tears streaming down her face.

Not far behind, Billy Adams kept one eye on the road and one on the vehicle three cars ahead. He didn't know where they were going or if there was anything he could do to help Millie when they got there. He just knew that he would find a way to get her away from Kurtz, come hell or high water. He took a deep breath. Time ticked away with the miles.

The sky was ashen, overcast, threatening rain. The spring air had turned chilly and dampness was creeping in. Billy Adams took off his peaked fishermen's hat. There was no sun to cause glare. In the heavy traffic, he was less afraid of losing Millie than arousing suspicion from Mr. Kurtz.

His eyes watched Millie being taken away with each mile they traveled. He had to keep the car within sight. Every muscle in his body was tense. There was a sour taste in Billy's mouth. What would happen when they reached their destination was anyone's guess.

Billy Adams seldom left Provincetown, except by boat. There was never any need. Truro, Wellfleet, and Eastham passed before his eyes in a blur. When they got to Orleans the car turned left onto Tonset Road. Large trees, long front lawns, and stately Cape homes gave way to woods and scrub brush as they continued down the country road. Billy was now heading east and if he kept going he would come to the Atlantic Ocean.

Adams watched the Chevrolet turn left into a private driveway. Billy took his foot off the accelerator and rolled passed a white Greek revival house with black shutters. Kurtz's car had stopped somewhere at the rear of the building, at the top of the wide drive. Billy caught a glimpse of a two-story barn. He was well past the house when he turned the car around and pulled off the road. Woods, shrub pine, and dense brush lined both sides of the roadway. There wasn't a building to be seen in either direction. He was less than a quarter of a mile from the house when he turned off the engine.

For twenty minutes Billy sat in the car looking at the road. Suddenly overwhelmed with a need to move, he got out of the truck and began to walk. A damp wind was bringing a storm.

As he neared the house he slipped into the woods. Drawn curtains made it impossible to see inside the house. He squat down and leaned against a tree. He had a view of the barn and the front of the house through the brush and trees.

Thirty minutes later the love-struck fisherman watched Joe Kurtz leave the house. He was alone. If the husband left in the car now, Billy would knock at the door and take Millie with him. He had no plan after that. But Joe Kurtz did not leave. Instead he headed for the barn where another man joined him. They entered a side door, leaving a bewildered fisherman trying to figure out what was going on in the barn.

Billy would not leave without his lover. He would wait. If she left with Kurtz, he would follow them. A time would come when he would catch her alone. During confession the priest had told Billy to give up the married woman, but he couldn't do it. He wanted her, to possess her, take her away and love her. He remembered all the stolen hours with vivid thoughts, her naked body next to him, her laughter at his silly jokes, and the plans they made. He could not fight the passion that grew within.

Resting against the tree, water dripping on his hat, he closed his eyes, said a prayer, and pictured Millie. He was dreaming of a better life.

The adrenaline that carried him here had ebbed, leaving a profound weariness. His head nodded against his chest. The sound of a motor woke him from his reverie. He was cold, wet, and full of doubt. A truck was coming up the driveway. The sky was growing lighter. It was just before sunrise, the twilight hours. A light over the front of the barn doors illuminated the men in the cab.

The fisherman watched the truck make a three point turn, so that the cargo hold was tight to the building, with the cab facing out. The headlamps were extinguished and Billy watched three men get out of the truck. The barn doors were still closed, possibly because of the rain, but they could be rolled apart to accept the truck. Two other men came from inside the barn to meet them. One was Joe Kurtz, the others he didn't recognize.

Unbeknownst to Billy, Chief Crowley was half- a- mile behind the truck, heading for the barn on Tonset Road. Crowley did not need to trail the smugglers to their destination. He knew where they were going, having been given directions and instructions by Detective Shiff. Their plans had taken shape in the chief's office after the fish fry on the previous night.

It had been decided that the chief would park next to an abandoned building and wait for Shiff and his buddies. They would be the first up the driveway. Crowley would follow.

"We are allowing the Provincetown Police to participate and are grateful for your help," the man in charge said. "But this sting is our operation." Crowley didn't mind not being the first in.

The chief had a good view in both directions and didn't take his eyes off the driveway. There was no other traffic. The first automobile sped past at 4:10 AM according to the chief's wristwatch. Two other vehicles followed. Every car had lights flashing. Crowley put the borrowed car in drive and brought up the rear.

Meanwhile, crouched low in the scrub brush, Billy couldn't take his eyes off the men, especially Joe Kurtz. He was drawn to the group, curious to know what they were doing. He crouched and then jogged closer to the house. The men were talking among themselves. Billy could hear the man in charge giving instructions.

"Put the cargo as far back as you can carry them. One man on each corner, they're heavier than they look," the man hollered at the others.

They were getting ready to unload whatever was in the back of the truck, when out of the fog four vehicles came speeding into the driveway. The men at the barn froze for a split second. A shout from one of the men at the back of the truck brought everyone out of the cargo hold. "Cops!" A second warning sounded. "Cops."

Red lights were flashing a stroboscopic light that blazed across the barn, the trees, and the house. The radiance throbbed against the dark night, pulsing out its meaning.

Billy was mesmerized. It was as if he were watching a movie. He stood up and began walking toward the house. He wanted to get to Millie. He heard the sirens wail and watched as men from the truck ran in different directions. He was reminded of rats fleeing a sinking ship. The barn, parking area, and back of the house were swept by the headlamps from the oncoming vehicles.

A demanding voice pierced the air. "This is the Police! Stay where you are!" The command through the megaphone continued, "This is the Police," he repeated. "Come out with your hands up! I repeat, come out with your hands up." The voice was absorbed into the wet forest. There was a moment of quiet before the first bullet shattered a windshield. Then all hell broke loose.

Billy sprinted for the house, arriving near the back steps. He dove for the ground into the brush, covering his head as the bullets began to fly. During a lull he looked up. Millie had stepped onto the back porch and was descending the steps. She had heard the voice demanding they give themselves up. She appeared in a daze as she moved slowly down the stairs.

Billy was on his feet, running toward her, calling her name. "Millie," he screamed. "Millie, get back." She turned to see Billy. Her eyes filled with confusion and panic.

Then Joe Kurtz stepped from the side of the cargo truck,

looking first at his wife and then at Billy. In the midst of this bewildering sight of cop cars, illegal contraband, and men with guns, Joe Kurtz began shrieking as if he'd come unglued, screaming obscenities at his wife. "You whore, you slut, you piece of trash. Is this the man?" He raised a gun and pointed it at his wife. "Is this the bastard?" Everyone in the yard could hear him. The cops couldn't see the man who was hollering because the truck blocked their view. No one moved. An eerie silence filled the space.

It happened so swiftly that no one had time to react. "No!" Billy screamed as he leaped forward, appearing to fly through the air. Joe Kurtz fired his gun. Both Billy and Mildred fell to the ground. The barrage of gunfire that followed sounded like fireworks on July 4th.

Chapter 32

Kurtz took refuge between the truck and the barn as the next salvo began. Keeping his head low, he then slipped into the barn. A hail of bullets swept across the yard. Shouts and orders could be heard over broken glass and popping gunfire.

Smith, Eddie and Joe were firing at random from inside the barn. The driver of the military vehicle ran into the woods as soon as he heard the word *Cops*. Not wanting to be mistaken for the enemy, Harry jumped behind a stack of cordwood on the left of the driveway when the flashing lights appeared.

Six men from the FBI, three Boston Police officers, a Boston Police Detective, one undercover cop, and one Provincetown Police Chief poured bullets into the barn as if trying to light it on fire. The smell of cordite hung in the air like cigar smoke over a poker table. Adrenaline was pumping, hands were shaking, and ears were ringing.

The Calvary arrived in the nick of time. If his superiors had not appeared when they did, the barn door would have been rolled open and Harry would have had to stall the men or to steal the vehicle, whatever it would take to keep the cargo from falling into the wrong hands. It could have created a siege.

A lull in gunshots was immediately filled by a voice calling out over a megaphone, repeating the words, "You are surrounded, come out with your hands up." The only reply was a bullet that whizzed past the cops' heads and went straight into the trees. Then another volley of gunfire racked the twilight.

The standoff didn't last long, only minutes, although to those present it felt like hours. Bullets struck police cars, metal against metal, followed by every officer using the side of the barn for target practice. The wooden structure looked like Swiss cheese. Everyone was either shooting or ducking their heads.

From somewhere inside the barn a voice began screaming, "I'm hit, I'm hit." high pitched like a terrified child. The man sounded deranged. It was useless for Smith and his boys to think of escape. They couldn't out run or out gun the police.

Inside the barn Smith was lying against the wall crying. There was blood running from his shoulder, down his arm, and onto the dirt floor. Eddie was slumped under a window looking at the empty chamber of his gun.

Kurtz had so much adrenaline in his system that his eyes were bulging like a frog. He was turning in all directions as if the answer to his dilemma was somewhere near, written on the barn walls.

Eddie shouted at his cohort, "I'm out of bullets. Give me your gun."

Smith didn't answer. He was crying.

"Not a chance," Kurtz hollered. He crouched low and headed for the side door.

As Joe slipped out, Eddie called after him, "You don't stand a chance, give it up." Kurtz didn't stop, but moved toward the back of the barn, hugging the wall. He slipped into the woods.

A deafening silence fell over the yard after the last bullet was fired. Nothing moved. Using a megaphone Detective Shiff again called, "You are surrounded. Come out with your hands up."

The air remained still. Raindrops could be heard striking leaves as they fell from the trees in a haphazard pattern giving off a musky smell when hitting the ground. The door to the barn began to slide sideways and from the darkened interior a voice shouted, "Don't shoot, I'm coming out." With hands held high above his head Eddie the Enforcer was the first to give up. He dropped his empty gun on the dirt floor of the barn.

Eddie stepped outside into the headlights of the three vehicles.

"Don't shoot, I'm unarmed." Eddie hollered. Uniformed officers appeared at his side, pushing him to the ground onto his knees.

"Where are the others?" Someone asked. Eddie didn't say another word. His arms were pulled behind his back and cuffs were secured to his wrists. Eddie was searched. Everything was removed from his pockets. The bully looked at the policeman with the gun pointed at him, smirked and then got into the back of the squad car.

The sky was turning from night to day, but no one noticed. Headlamps illuminated the area like a movie set from a James Cagney film. Crowley moved quickly, skirting the edge of the war zone. He went directly to the lovers.

They appeared to be in some kind of embrace, lying together in the wet grass at the foot of the steps. Crowley got down on his knees beside them. Billy's body was covering Millie. One arm was wrapped around her, the other flung out to the side. Neither moved.

The chief placed his hand on the fisherman's neck, felt a pulse and said, "Billy, Billy can you hear me?" He then yelled across the yard. "Get an ambulance."

Blood seeped from underneath the two prone figures, mixing together as if they formed a brotherhood pact. The rain and the blood ran in rivulets across dirt. Crowley put his ear close to the couple. He heard breathing. He gently rolled Billy off Mildred Kurtz. Blood stuck to their shirts and upper torsos. Crowley couldn't tell who was bleeding. He quickly surmised that they both were.

"You'll be ok, hold on," the chief choked out the words. "The ambulance is on its way, you're going to be ok." Crowley's voice got louder. He kept repeating, "Millie, can you hear me? You're going to be ok." Crowley took a handkerchief from his pocket and pushed it to the skin that was oozing blood from a wound in

Mildred Kurtz's upper chest. He held it firmly in place. Her eyes fluttered but she did not respond when he called her name.

Shiff appeared at his side. "Ambulance will be here in a few minutes, it's on the way." Sirens could be heard in the distance. A second Boston Officer appeared next to Shiff, ready to help.

"Both have wounds, both bleeding. Please, stay with them. I've got to get Kurtz." He looked at both policemen. "Here, hold this, put pressure, but not too much, she's small." He showed Shiff the wounds on both victims.

"I have to do this." He got up and ran without further explanation.

Crowley had glimpsed Joe Kurtz leaving the side door of the barn. He knew the killer had made his way to the back of the barn. Instinct took Crowley to the path on the opposite side, hoping to catch up with Kurtz before he had time to slip into the woods. Light from the rising sun filled the sky with a mellow, muted yellow light. A row of lilac bushes along the edge of the building left behind a sad sweet smell as the chief brushed by.

Sweat on Crowley's forehead fell in drops, but he didn't feel them. The bushes offered little in the way of concealment, so Crowley moved quickly along the side of the wooden structure. The chief saw a small clearing and then the tree line. He listened as he looked around.

The snap of a branch caused the chief to turn. Harry appeared from the other side of the barn. At the same time Kurtz stepped from the tree line. It happened fast. Kurtz turned to Crowley who was only a few yards away.

Both guns sounded simultaneously. The men looked at each other across a twenty-foot space. One man looked surprised, the other woeful. Time slowed. Kurtz fell to his knees. The duel was over.

A shout came from the other side of the barn, "Chief, you ok?" Harry was pressing himself against the wall. He repeated, "Chief, are you ok?" The morning light glowed against the mist, an eerie fusion of golden sunrise and leftover rain.

Crowley lifted his hand as if it were made of lead. He was glad to hear Harry's voice. "I'm ok." The chief shook his head as if he didn't believe what he said. "What about you?"

Harry couldn't smile, but he tried to lighten the scene. "Even with all the bullets flying it seems I was missed."

Crowley pointed across the lawn. "I don't think Kurtz was as lucky. He's behind that tree at the edge of the yard. You go left. I'll go right. I saw him go down, but I don't know how bad he is. He still has the gun, so be on guard."

Within seconds they were standing over Joe Kurtz. There was blood oozing from a chest wound and red foam seeping from the corners of his mouth. He was leaning against a tree with his eyes closed, appearing asleep. A gun lay on the ground next to him. Harry picked it up.

Joe Kurtz opened his eyes and looked at Crowley and then at Harry. Surprise flashed across the man's face. Then his eyes sagged with weariness as if he were longing for sleep. The chief thought he looked like a puppet without a puppeteer to move the strings. The mist was rising, promising a warm June day.

Crowley knelt, put his hand on the man's shoulder, and bent his head close to Kurtz's mouth. "I should have known better," Kurtz whispered. They turned out to be his last words. Crowley wasn't sure if Kurtz meant Harry, his wife Mildred, or trying to smuggle guns for the Nazis, maybe all three. Blood was pooling around the dying man.

The chief remained bent over Kurtz like a priest giving absolution. Crowley became aware that he was holding his breath. Precious seconds passed. The chief waited for more words. There were none. Crowley checked for a pulse, he looked into the dilated pupils, then slowly stood and faced Harry. "He's dead. There's no breath, pupils are fixed and dilated."

Harry looked at the body, then Crowley, and nodded. "We'd better let Shiff know what's up," Harry said. The two policemen began walking side by side, back to the front of the barn.

There was an orderly sense of chaos throughout the scene when Harry and Crowley arrived at the parking area. The Orleans fire and rescue trucks had arrived. Men in various uniforms were walking around, amazed by what they were looking at. Bullet holes were everywhere, windshields shattered, plainclothes agents huddled at the rear of a truck that was parked in front of the barn. The hood, windshield, and both fenders had holes.

Two ambulance attendants were loading a stretcher into the back of a van that looked like a bakery truck with a red cross painted on the side. Mr. Smith was strapped to a board. The barn doors had been thrown open. Men were searching the grounds around the barn and house.

A uniformed officer pointed at the house with the black shutters. "All secure in the house. We found one woman hiding in an upstairs closet," the policeman told Shiff. "Said her name was Rose Smith. I put her in the back of the Orleans cruiser."

Detective Shiff nodded to the officer and then headed for the two men who were coming from behind the barn. Shiff crossed the dirt yard, hollering as he went. "I heard the shots. Are you ok?" He kept walking toward the two officers. "An ambulance has already left with the couple," Shiff told Harry and Crowley.

The three men were standing in a group when Shiff continued, "The ambulance driver couldn't tell me much. They are both alive, but have lost a lot of blood." Shiff put his hand on Crowley's shoulder. "I take it you know the couple?"

The Provincetown Police Chief nodded. "The woman is Mildred Kurtz, wife of Joe Kurtz. The boy is Billy Adams, a fisherman from Provincetown, I've known him his whole life." Crowley took a deep breath.

The three men looked around the yard, appearing

overwhelmed for a moment. The rain had stopped and the sun was breaking through the fog. A man in boots and oil coat was directing a fire truck that was backing down the driveway. Shiff continued, "Things are secured here, I was about to come looking for you. What about Kurtz?"

Harry said, "He'll need the Medical Examiner. He's dead."

The Boston detective continued, "Mr. Smith, his wife, and the one they call Eddie are in custody. All our men are accounted for. I say it was a success." The Boston Detective took a deep breath, without a cigarette in his mouth.

Crowley nodded his head toward the barn. "Kurtz is in back of the barn, at the edge of the woods. You can't miss him." The Provincetown Police Chief looked at the ground like a schoolboy who didn't want to admit his part in the episode. He continued. "The short version is that it came down to either him or me." Shiff looked at Harry who nodded his head in agreement, but did not speak.

Crowley continued, "I'll give you my written statements when I get back to the office."

"The chief didn't have a choice," Harry said. "I've got Kurtz's gun, two bullets left." He handed it to his boss.

Shiff pocketed the pistol and then put his hand on the chief's shoulder. "I'll see that Kurtz is taken care of. He'll go to Pocasset to the ME. I'll need a written statement from both of you by tomorrow afternoon." They walked together toward the chief's borrowed car.

"I'm going to stop at the hospital before I head back to Provincetown," Crowley said. "I want to see how they are. And the doctors will need information about the couple. You've got your hands full here. We can meet later in my office."

The Provincetown Police Chief looked at the car that belonged to Joe Duarte. The windshield was gone. There was a huge hole on the passenger side window, and one headlamp was missing.

Crowley asked Shiff what was going to happen to the man in the back of the state police car.

"The fellow wants to make a deal," Detective Shiff gave a small chuckle. "I doubt that's going to happen. We'll get some good information out of that one. He's a bully, now squealing like a pig."

"Eddie the Enforcer, not so much enforcing now," Harry said.

Shiff lit a Lucky Strike and smiled. "The other one, they call Smitty, supposed to be the boss. He's the one they loaded into the ambulance. He's got a bullet in his shoulder. They tell me he'll live. He was crying like a baby? His brown shirt with a swastika was covered in dirt and blood. Just a dirty little Nazi." The Boston detective shook his head and inhaled the cigarette smoke.

"The driver of the truck ran into the woods. My guys tell me he won't get far, all marsh and dunes around here." Shiff's speech had picked up speed as he related what he knew. "A wireless was sent to the Coast Guard about the *Maura Marie*. They'll get her. And before I forget, I want to talk to that fisherman who owns the *Santina*, as soon as possible. Pick him up when you get back. I'll be in your office tomorrow afternoon."

The Provincetown Police Chief took two deep breaths as if trying to replace the smell of cordite and blood with fresh air. He got into the beat up truck, started the engine, and headed for Hyannis. Crowley looked in the rear view mirror at the bullet-ridden barn and the truck full of guns. He felt his eyes stinging. He pictured Kurtz, the look of surprise in his eyes before the life had gone out of them. Crowley press down on the accelerator as soon as the car hit paved road.

Chapter 33

Everywhere Billy looked he saw white, as if he were inside an igloo like the one he and his pals dug into the snow when he was eight years old. His chest was tightly wrapped. His arm was strapped to a board that was tied to the bedrail. Billy groaned. Chief Crowley had been sitting in a chair next to the bed for two hours. The policeman stood when he heard the patient moan. The fisherman's eyes opened.

"I was hoping you'd wake up while I was here," Crowley said. "They tell me you are going to be ok." The chief wasn't smiling. A crease formed on his forehead as he pulled his eyebrows together.

"We need to talk." He waited to let this sink in. Billy's eyes focused on the chief. Crowley continued, "I know this won't be easy, but I need you to tell me the truth about what happened to Frank White." The chief spoke slowly making sure the patient understood. "I know Mr. White came looking for Joe Kurtz. Joe wasn't home. You need to tell me what happened." Chief Crowley waited.

Billy closed his eyes. When he opened them he said, "Is Millie alright?" When the chief nodded yes, Billy continued. "What has Millie told you?'"

"I'm sorry Billy. I need to hear about this from you, in your words. I need you to tell me what happened and I need the truth." The chief was calm. He waited for the injured man to speak, to tell the real story about what had happened on that fateful night.

"I killed him. I didn't mean to," he blurted out. Billy started to cry. "I went to her house. The light was on. I went around back, but she didn't answer my tap. She should have opened the door right away." He stopped speaking. Tears were covering his cheeks. Billy made a wet slushy noise. The wounded man looked at Crowley with misery in his eyes.

The chief stood motionless as he spoke. "Ok, Billy, go slow. I need you to tell me everything. I know this is difficult." The chief gave the fisherman a handkerchief. Billy sobbed into it then blew his nose.

All the hurt in the world seemed to be in his eyes. "When she didn't come to the door, I let myself in. I heard her pleading for him to stop, crying and screaming at him to *please let her go.* I can still hear her, the fear in her voice." Billy stopped speaking and began crying again.

"I didn't mean to kill him. I just wanted to stop him. The scissors were lying there, next to her sewing basket. I don't remember picking them up. It happened so fast." Billy took a mournful breath and sighed. "He died so quickly. I didn't mean to kill him. He was a monster. I had to stop him. I had to."

The words seemed to exhaust him. He closed his eyes, turned his head away, sobbing. He had been living with this burden. The fisherman wasn't finished speaking. His words were just audible to the police chief. "He didn't even hear me come into the room. He was bent over her. The bastard had his pants around his ankles." Billy used the handkerchief to muffle his sob.

A line from Shakespeare's *King Lear* came to Crowley's mind: *I am a man more sinned against than sinning.* Crowley knew the law. He also knew what justice meant and sometimes they are not the same. "I don't want you to talk to anyone else about this. You understand? Not one word," the chief's voice was firm. Billy grunted a yes.

The chief faced the window and looked out on a bright June morning. He could see the harbor and the fishing boats as they danced on their moorings.

Again he pictured the moment when Joe Kurtz fired his gun, Billy jumping in front of Millie, her look of surprise. By some strange twist of fate the bullet passed through Billy and then hit Millie. The surgeon told the chief that if Billy hadn't jumped in from of Mildred she would have died for sure.

Crowley stood next to the bed. His hands touched the cold bed rail. He leaned closer to the fisherman. "You're going to be alright." Chief Crowley turned to leave, but stopped. "One more thing, Billy. What did you do with his personal effects and the scissors?"

"I threw them all into the sea," the fisherman said, "along with the rug we wrapped him in. I took them out to the boat that night and dropped everything overboard three miles from land."

A nurse came into the room to give Billy an injection. He was asleep almost immediately.

The chief had one more stop to make. His feet on the stairs sounded like a drum, slow, heavy, and echoing against the walls as he climbed to the third floor surgical unit. He took a deep breath and opened the door that had the name Mildred Kurtz next to it. She was asleep. Her left arm and shoulder were in a plaster cast hanging from a triangular frame across the top of the bed. She was swaddled in white sheets like a newborn baby. An IV ran into her right arm. A nurse looked up as he entered the hushed room. When the chief showed his identification, she nodded and told him he could stay a few minutes.

Mildred looked like a child. Her innocence spoke to him. Her dark hair flowing around her head reminded Crowley of a bird, a raven perhaps. He did not wake her, did not try to talk to her. Crowley felt a heavy weight lifting from his chest when the nurse told him that with rest, care, and time, she was going to be okay.

Before he left the hospital he called the station to let Lewis know that he was on his way home. "I'll be back in the office in an hour," Crowley told Lewis. "We can catch up then."

During the drive, the Chief relived the early morning scene. It felt as if his heart had stopped when he watched Billy and Mildred hit the ground. The sight of the blood pooling under the couple had brought an anger that he didn't know existed in him. All he could think about was to get Joe Kurtz and bring him to justice.

When confronted, Joe Kurtz looked at him with hatred in his eyes. Crowley had reacted with ferocity, without thinking. It was a physical reaction like he had been taught in the military. The chief now wondered about what he was feeling when he raised the gun and fired? Were the chief's feelings a mirror of Kurtz's own hate? Surely it takes hate to kill a man. He didn't have a choice and he didn't hesitate. Nevertheless, it had taken a toll. James Crowley felt unclean as if there were a stain on his soul.

Without the car's windshield the wind was a tempest against him, whipping through his hair. He felt exposed. The inrush of air forced him awake. Occasionally his face was blasted by sand and he had to momentarily close his eyes. It stung. It reminded him that he could feel pain, he was alive, and that was a good thing.

The drive to Provincetown from Hyannis gave him plenty of time to think. An idea was forming. Mildred Kurtz wasn't an innocent woman, but she didn't deserve what had happened to her. Where was the justice for her?

The chief arrived at the station late morning. Lewis had been there all night. He dozed on a cot in the cell while waiting for news. The office smelled of coffee. The young policeman had the phone resting on his left shoulder, a pencil in his right hand writing, while he spoke. "Oh, hold on. He's just come in," he said.

Crowley held up his hand signaling Lewis to wait. "What a night," he said. "I'll take the call in my office and I could use a cup of coffee." Crowley made his way down the narrow cement corridor. He took off his jacket and sat heavily in his chair. He yawned. The adrenaline had worn off and life was beginning to catch up to him. He picked up the phone. "Crowley."

"We got 'um and we got what they were delivering too." Shiff was talking, but not as fast as usual. Crowley didn't interrupt him.

Shiff continued, "The crates were full of rifles, dynamite, bullets, and a few of the newer type of hand grenades. The feds will follow up on this."

Shiff was on a roll. "The items are considered dangerous to the public health and welfare and come under the laws covering smuggling. The penalties date back centuries, having been used to hang men. Anyone involved can receive fines and be imprisoned." Crowley could hear Shiff take a puff on a cigarette. "I can't talk now, I'll see you tomorrow," the Boston policeman said.

Crowley didn't have time to ask questions. Shiff hung up without saying goodbye.

Lewis came into the office with two steaming mugs. When they were seated Crowley told Lewis about what had occurred. "Mildred Kurtz and Billy Adams are in the hospital and will live." Crowley yawned and pulled off his hat. "I'd like you to find any family they have and explain where they are." Lewis nodded.

Crowley recapped the night for Lewis, going into detail about the shoot-out at the barn, Joe Kurtz shooting Billy and Mildred with one bullet, and the shot that brought down Kurtz. But Crowley did not tell Lewis what Billy had confessed to or what Kurtz had said to him as he lay dying. It was his sin of omission.

The chief was wrestling with his conscience. Vague murmurings from somewhere deep inside were bubbling to the surface. A web of intrigue was taking root. Crowley didn't know how he felt about it or what he would do about it.

"Did you know that Aristotle in 300 B.C. wrote: *the law is reason free from passion.* It's a quote I picked up at the Police Academy." Crowley said. "But the words *mercy and justice* are not a part of it."

"Billy Adams is not a bad person," the chief continued. "He's a hard worker, is community spirited, and is liked by all who know him." Crowley looked at Lewis who was staring at him as if trying to understand what the chief was getting at. Crowley shook his head and smiled. "He just fell in love with a married woman."

"Right," Lewis said, "And sounds like he's paying for it now."

The two men sat at the big desk, sipping coffee and talking about the days leading to the early morning gunfight. The weeks had been filled with questions, puzzles, intrigue, love and hate. "And it all came to an abrupt end," Crowley said. He lit his pipe. "This has been quite a night, or should I say morning."

Lewis stood up and picked up the two empty cups. "It's good that not one police officer was hurt. We can be thankful for that." The chief nodded his head as Lewis left the office.

Crowley stared at his murder board. He began removing the cards one by one. He held the card bearing the name Joe Kurtz. He couldn't wipe the hatred in Joe Kurtz's eyes from his thoughts. He saw that look twice. The first time when he fired at his wife Mildred and again when he raised his gun to kill the chief. Crowley wondered where such feelings come from. There was no doubt in the police chief's mind that Joe Kurtz was a killer. He was a man in league with the devil and he had a twisted sense of who should run the world. And yet, Crowley wrestled with his conscience.

The phone rang and Crowley picked it up. "Provincetown Police Department," he said, sounding weary. He immediately recognized the voice on the other end.

"Hi chief. I just wanted to say thanks and to let you know that I won't be back in Provincetown for a while. Lot's of loose ends to tie up and my boss doesn't want me showing my face. He said he doesn't want me tainted by hanging out with the police chief." They both laughed. Harry continued, "If you are ever in Boston, look me up. I'll cook you a nice spaghetti dinner."

"I may take you up on that," Crowley said. "And thanks for all your help. I believe we've closed both cases, smuggling and murder."

Harry frowned, unseen on the other end of the phone line,

"Are you talking about Frank White? As far as I know no one has confessed to killing him. It is my understanding that Smitty and Eddie have clammed up, asked for lawyers and have not confessed to anything. So tell me what I don't know." Harry waited.

The time for mercy and justice had come. "Remember when I bent to listen to Kurtz before he died? Well he confessed to killing the salesman, said he was defending his wife from a sexual attack. Came home and caught him. Killed him with the scissors." It surprised the chief to hear the words come from his mouth. He could not remember ever telling a lie, not to anyone. A feeling of guilt and shame came over him, and yet on a deeper level a lightness of spirit stirred beneath. He was glad Harry couldn't see his face.

Crowley continued, "I was a bit dazed at the scene. I was only thinking about Billy and Mrs. Kurtz." The chief was committed. "As far as the Provincetown Police Department is concerned Frank White's murder case is closed. As for smuggling, treason, shooting at federal agents, and attempted murder," Crowley paused, "I have no doubt that your boss and his bosses will continue to safeguard our country against those who would oppress us."

Harry jumped into the conversation. "Joe Kurtz was a slime ball. We witnessed what he was capable of. If he had had his way, his wife, the young fisherman, you and me would all be dead. He played with fire and got what he deserved." Harry finished with, "And it warms the cockles of my heart to know that both Smith and Eddie are now behind bars."

They said goodbye. Harry added that they should keep in touch. It was unlikely they're paths would cross again anytime soon. Crowley began to put the phone back in its' cradle but then he placed his finger on the O and dialed. The operator asked, "What number?"

The chief didn't hesitate, "1394, please." It rang three times.

"Alter residence. How may I help you?" He was so pleased to hear her voice that he didn't say anything. She said, "Hello?"

"Hi, Susan, it's me, James. I was wondering if I could see you?" There was no talk of death or murder in their conversation. "I'd like you to meet some friends of mine, more like family, really. Eleanor and Manny Diogo, they run the ship chandlery in the center of town. Do you know them?" Their conversation went on for a few minutes and arrangements were made for the following week.

Chapter 34

Crawley placed the phone into the cradle on his desk. He sighed and whispered, "And miles to go before I sleep." The chief had just enough energy left to finish what needed to be done. He picked up his hat, stopped at the front desk and said, "Lewis, let's go. We need to pick up Salvador. We'll try the boat first." The two men headed out into the sunshine.

Tied near the end of Fishermen's Wharf on this sunny June day was the schooner *Gertrude L Thibaud*. The explorer Admiral Donald B McMillan was provisioning the ship for another trip north. The newspaper proclaimed that this time he was traveling to Baffin Island, a large island belonging to Canada located at the mouth of Hudson Bay.

Everyone in town knew that McMillan married his wife Miriam in 1935, and that they lived in a small cape house on Commercial Street. Their home contained a Narwhal tusk hanging on the wall, a stuffed Polar Bear that stood with its head touching the ceiling, and cabinets filled with mementoes from his Artic travels.

Crowley passed the Admiral's vessel. Their eyes were fixed on the *Santina*. The boat was tied to the pier where it had unloaded the confiscated cargo. The two officers stepped aboard. Crowley wrapped his knuckles on the doghouse, the outcropping that led to the living quarters. The chief called, "Captain Salvador I'd like a word with you."

The fisherman appeared from below with a cigarette dangling from his mouth. He recognized the policemen and the smile on Salvador's face changed completely.

"We need you to come with us," Crowley said. "We have a few questions we'd like to ask you."

"Ah nuts," came the reply. "Whatever it is, I don't know nothing." The fisherman said.

"You won't be giving me any reason to put handcuffs on you, right?" Lewis asked.

The fishermen said he'd come quietly.

Lewis drove. Crowley sat in back with Salvador. The two men had spoken on occasion, at fishermen's meetings, at town hall meetings, and on the street. The chief wished there was a way he could help the fisherman instead of arresting him, but there was no way out. Salvador was looking at hard time. His boat would be confiscated and who knew what the FBI had in store for him.

The chief turned in the seat. "There is a Boston detective named Charles Shiff that will be here tomorrow. He wants to talk to you about what you were up to last night." The prisoner let out a groan. Crowley continued, "Until he gets here you are to remain in my custody. You don't have to say anything and you have the right to a lawyer." The chief looked at the fisherman. "This is serious. You should be thinking about how you want to spend the next ten years of your life."

He let that hang in the air before continuing. "It would be in your best interests to cooperate with Detective Shiff." Nothing else was said during the ride. The door to the cell closed with a bang. Crowley tuned the key in the lock. Salvador sat on the cot, put his head in his hands, and moaned.

Crowley left his office. On his way out he said to Lewis, "My ears are still ringing. I need food and some sleep. I'll be back in a few hours. We can take turns keeping an eye on the detainee. Please call the Mayflower Café and order a meal for Salvador and one for yourself. Put it on the department tab."

He was closing the door when he heard Lewis holler, "Yes, sir. You can count on me."

The following day Detective Shiff arrived at police headquarters with a man. Chief Crowley put out his hand. "Joe Amaral, still working for the Federal Bureau of Investigation? Good to see you," the chief said.

The three law enforcement agents hadn't seen each other in six months. They had worked together in a similar capacity, a murder, smuggling, and the rescue of Mary Diogo, daughter to Chief Crowley's best friend. But that was in the past.

Crowley shook hands with both men. "I'll bring in the fisherman. He's had all night to think about his predicament. He refused a lawyer, said he didn't have the money to pay John Snow."

Crowley returned with Salvador. His hands were cuffed in front, his head bent, appearing resigned to his fate. Chief Crowley told the fisherman to take a seat at the table in the back of the room. The corkboard with all the file cards, notes, and folders pertaining to the murder had been removed. Salvador was told to sit.

Shiff began. He spoke softly to Salvador. "You know why we're here?" When Salvador didn't reply the Boston policeman continued. "We have been watching you and your boat. Saturday night you unloaded crates that contained guns and ammunition. If we were at war it would be viewed as an act of treason." He let the words hang in the air. "As it stands, you are looking at smuggling charges."

The Boston cop held an unlit cigarette in his hand. "We have a witness who will state in court that you brought that shipment into the country on your fishing vessel. You are looking at serious charges, jail time."

The fisherman looked up at the three law enforcement officers. "What do you want?" Salvador asked. "I figured you must want something or I'd already be in chains at the Charles Street Jail."

Shiff didn't waste time. He continued, "The crates are now in our possession. We want the ship that brought them in. We want Mr. Smith, Eddie, and any other person you had contact with. That's where you come in."

He paused to give the prisoner time to digest what had been said.

Agent Amaral spoke for the first time. "In return for your testimony against the captain of the freighter, Mr. Smith, and his pals, the United States Government will grant you a pardon and immunity from prosecution in this case."

"You mean I walk away, keep my boat, no jail time?" Salvador stopped and looked across the room at Chief Crowley as if he were the only one in the room that he trusted. Crowley's head gave a nod. "I want it in writing," Salvador said.

Amaral and Shiff looked at each other and grinned. "First things first," Shiff said. "I also want a sworn statement to the same facts from your crewman. That will come later."

After an hour of questioning the FBI agent and the Boston detective stood. "Captain Salvador has agreed to come with us." Shiff said.

Chief Crowley halted the prisoner by stepping in front of him. "If I ever hear about you being involved in anything like this again I swear I'll see that they throw the book at you. You won't get a second chance. Are we clear?" Chief Crowley asked. Salvador nodded.

There was a knock, the door opened, and two men in dark suits stepped in. An FBI Agent took Salvador by the arm. "Then we'll leave you," Agent Amaral said. "Captain Salvador will be under the government's care for a awhile." The four men headed for the waiting car.

The door closed, vibrating the glass at the top. Shiff walked to the chair facing the chief's desk and sat heavily. "He seems willing to cooperate. He'll have to make a statement of his complicity and give testimony before a grand jury. He's a smart guy. He'll be back fishing in a couple of months." Shiff bent his head back, looking up at the ceiling. "He's a tough cookie."

After a short pause the Boston Detective added, "He's getting off light."

Shiff continued, "The FBI is going to have a field day with this one. It'll keep them busy for months. They're anxious to talk to Salvador." The Boston detective paused. He had been running on coffee and cigarettes for twenty-four hours. "If the feds like what he has to say they'll go easy on him."

Shiff had served in the military and prided himself as a defender of America. "We've got terrorists and anti-American propaganda right now, right here in the good old US of A. Let's hope we can stop this train in its tracks." The feeling that the war in Europe was overflowing onto American soil was something that was talked about in offices, around the pubs, and in the homes of its citizens.

Shiff quoted President Franklin Roosevelt, "*When peace has been broken anywhere, the peace of all countries everywhere is in danger.*" Both policemen sat quietly then Shiff regained his composure and finished summing up the case.

"The man in charge calls himself Smith, but his fingerprints have identified him as a German nationalist named Herman Eisling. He's in protective custody at Boston City Hospital. The bullet wound was just a scratch, passed right through a muscle."

He let that sink in before continuing, "Eddie, we believe fits the description of a man wanted by the New York City Police for questioning in a murder case where a man was thrown from the twelfth floor of a downtown hotel." He paused. Crowley could hear him breathing.

"The driver of the truck was found wandering the beach out near Nauset Lighthouse, lost, wet and hungry. Seems he walked across the marsh, ended up on the beach and didn't know which way to go. HA," Shiff grunted. "When he was picked up he looked like a Halloween scarecrow. He's been talking his head off."

Shiff paused to take another puff from the Lucky Strike.

"Listen, I don't want Harry's name brought up. No need to put our boy in harm's way. As far as anyone is concerned he was arrested along with the rest of the gang."

Shiff picked up his jacket and walked toward the office door, stopped, and turned. "And by-the-way, congratulations on closing the murder case. I got the news from Harry. I'm surprised you didn't tell me when we were at the barn." Both men paused to think about the shoot out. "Or you could have said something when I spoke to you on the phone yesterday. I'd rather have heard it from you," The Boston Detective said.

"You never gave me a chance. You hung up before I could get a word in edgewise. And you know yourself that my mind was on other things out at the barn. I think I was in shock." It was now the truth. Crowley held the door open for the Boston policeman and looked him in the eye. They shook hands. A Bible quote came to Crowley's mind, *"Fear God, for he shall bring every work into judgment, with every secret thing, whether it be good, or whether it be evil,"* but the chief did not utter a word.

"Well yes, with all the confusion, I can understand." The Boston Detective smiled. "And just between us I'm glad it turned out to be that Nazi bastard. Let's hope I don't hear from you for a long time. And when we do meet again, it will be when I'm on vacation."

The door closed. The room seemed unusually quiet as if all sound had been sucked out. Crowley felt very alone.

The chief pulled out his notepad and made a list.

#1. Pick up Ernie Thomas, Salvador's crewman

#2. See the farmer next door to Mrs. Gracie re: gun fire

#3. Ask Lewis to pick up a baby outfit for Mrs. Oliver.

#4. See Joe Duarte about fixing the borrowed car. Pay?

#5. Write up report for selectman.

#6. See about getting Lewis a raise.

#7. Check with Manny and Eleanor Diogo about having dinner with him at the Pilgrim House. Ask Susan and set date.

He closed the pad and picked up the phone. He asked the operator to put him through to Doctor Rice's office. Mrs. Rice answered and said the doctor was with a patient and that she'd have him call the chief in a few minutes.

While he waited, Crowley began writing the report. It would go to the County Medical Office, to Detective Shiff in Boston along with a letter of thanks, and one copy for his records. He wrote down the details, placing the blame squarely on Joe Kurtz. Mr. Kurtz found the victim, Frank White, assaulting his wife. Mr. Kurtz stabbed Frank White in the back with scissors that he later threw into the Atlantic Ocean. Mr. Kurtz confessed to the killing as he lay dying at the rear of a barn on Tonset Road in Orleans.

Chief Crowley signed the letters and addressed the envelopes.

He felt no remorse. There were only three people who knew the truth. There was no wish to recall the event. It seemed a practical ending. Crowley's thoughts about surviving brutality and violence kept the pen moving across the paper. He was still writing when the phone rang. He picked it up. "Crowley here."

"Are you sick?" The physician asked.

"I thought you might like to know that the Frank White murder case is closed. Joe Kurtz confessed as he lay dying." The chief started coughing. He cleared his throat and took a sip of cold coffee "I'll tell you the story when you can slow down long enough to hear it."

The doctor laughed. Crowley hung up the phone.

Late that night, unable to unwind or sleep, the chief drove back to Cape Cod Hospital. He told Billy Adams what his report would say. "Mildred has suffered enough," Crowley said. He explained to the fisherman that he didn't want to see her dragged through courts having to explain what happened to her. "I believe you acted in a moment of passion, without regard for anything except Mildred. And I believe you are not a murderer, at least not in your heart."

Crowley spoke softly, "I've written a report. Mildred will have to sign it when she's out of the hospital, but there will be no court hearing. You must never talk about this to anyone, ever. This will be the end of it."

Billy started to cry, but the Chief wasn't finished. "I think you should take Mildred away from here. You've got your fishing business and I'm sure you'd be welcome in New Bedford or Boston."

Billy said, "We'll go to Gloucester. I have family there."

The Chief put into words what the two men were thinking. "There is no turning back. We will have to live with our consciences and let God grant forgiveness." The chief put his hand on Billy's shoulder and said goodbye.